"Just tell me your real name."

Of its own volition, Jacob's head dipped. His chin brushed just beside her temple. He filled his lungs and senses with another lingering breath of her hair, of her. "I can help you through whatever's going on. Running never solved anything."

Easing back a step, she placed the money on the table before turning on her heels. "Here, this should be enough to cover my phone call to the Tacoma Police Department." Dee cleared the doorway before he could close his mouth.

Regret and frustration jockeyed for dominance in Jacob's testosterone-fogged brain. Why was his gut twisting into knots over this woman he'd just met? Why would someone running from the law call the cops? She wouldn't.

Could she have been telling the truth after all?

Damn.

Jacob sprinted after her, right back into the storm.

Dear Reader,

Welcome to the next installment of my WINGMEN
WARRIORS series!

Amnesia stories have long been a favorite of readers
and of mine, as well. I tinkered with the idea of amnesia in
Awaken to Danger, when the heroine lost one night of her
life. As I was writing it, I couldn't let go of the notion of
someone losing all memories while stranded in the middle
of nowhere. On an emotional level, how can a person know
themselves without any sense of the choices made before?
Even on a practical level, the whole world becomes a
landmine when someone isn't aware of allergies, preexisting
medical conditions, even food preferences. (For a person
like me, with plenty of food aversions, this alone became a
daunting notion!)

Furthermore, with so little self-knowledge, how then would
that person be able to recognize love? That part seemed
simpler to answer. The heart's capacity to love is timeless
as well as boundless. So welcome to Dee and Jacob's story
as they discover love at a time when Dee has no memory of
her past and Jacob wrestles with the possibility of leaving
his military identity behind.

Thank you for reading!

All the best,

Catherine Mann
www.catherinemann.com

CATHERINE MANN

Out of Uniform

Silhouette®

Romantic

SUSPENSE

 SILHOUETTE BOOKS

ISBN-13: 978-0-373-27571-7
ISBN-10:   0-373-27571-4

OUT OF UNIFORM

Books by Catherine Mann

Silhouette Romantic Suspense

Joint Forces #1293
Explosive Alliance #1346
The Captive's Return #1388
Awaken to Danger #1401
Fully Engaged #1440
Holiday Heroes #1487
 "Christmas at His Command"
Out of Uniform #1501

*Wingmen Warriors

Silhouette Desire

Baby, I'm Yours #1721
*Under the
 Millionaire's Influence* #1787
*The Executive's
 Surprise Baby* #1837

CATHERINE MANN

writes contemporary military romances, a natural fit, since she's married to her very own USAF research source. Prior to publication, Catherine graduated with a BA in fine arts: theatre from the College of Charleston, and received her master's degree in theatre from UNC Greensboro. Now a RITA® Award winner, Catherine finds following her aviator husband around the world with four children, a beagle and a tabby in tow offers her endless inspiration for new plots. Learn more about her work, as well as her adventures in military life, by visiting her Web site: www.catherinemann.com, or contact her at P.O. Box 41433, Dayton, OH 45441.

To my dear sister-in-law, Melissa Mann, who has come to visit us everywhere we've lived, no matter how cold! I love you!

Chapter 1

"Hell's bells, here comes Betty Crocker in a bustier." Tech Sergeant Jacob "Mako" Stone pitched his remote control onto his family's motel check-in counter and took a second look at the walking contradiction in the parking lot.

Washington winter winds whipped sleet and snow sideways, the icy sheet parting before encircling a shivering woman. She stumbled, righted her spiked heels and hobbled toward the main office of the run-down motel where Jacob had grown up.

Now, he only planned to stick around long enough to get his teenage—orphaned—sister's life in order before he returned to his career as an Air Force in-flight mechanic. Okay, so he was technically on sick leave while his arm recovered from a line-of-duty bullet. But he hoped to be back in his flight suit, tooling around the sky with his C-17 buddies in two more weeks.

Fourteen days certain to be jam-packed settling his sister's life—and his old man's near-bankrupt "estate."

That alone should be enough for his plate. Pulling his gaze off the woman, Jacob adjusted his healing arm in the sling with a wince and shifted his attention to the *Dr. Phil* rerun again in hopes the shrink could offer up some insights on how to help a teenager with an infant get her life on track. Fixing his sister's situation seemed harder than keeping a multimillion-dollar military aircraft in smooth working order.

Still, curiosity hauled his gaze right back to the parking lot as the woman's coat flapped open. Her slinky dress, racy-red lingerie peeking free with each stormy gust, just didn't match the Junior League face.

She huddled inside her coat and started up the office steps. She probably needed to call a friend, and the phones were out.

The woman wrapped her arms around her willowy body and tucked her head into the storm. She must be from room sixteen, since his only other customer had been a horse rancher who'd checked out an hour ago. Jacob hadn't seen the woman up close when she'd arrived the night before. She'd been slumped asleep in the car while "Mr. Smith" had paid cash for their room.

Jacob glanced toward the parking spaces. Mr. Smith's

white Suburban was long gone, snow already piling in the tire ruts.

Damn.

Sympathy and frustration stuttered through Jacob like the bullets that had come his way during a simple assignment hauling a congressional entourage around Europe. Apparently this woman's wild night out on the tiny town hadn't unfolded as planned.

Double damn. Already he could feel warrior instincts honed in bloody battle zones stirring to life within him.

Jacob pushed to his feet, snagging his remote control from beside the television. Extending his arm, he thumbed the remote, silencing *Dr. Phil*.

He might not be wearing his uniform, and the woman may not need his help. But that wouldn't stop him from throwing himself in the middle of her problems when she came through the door. The only way to ensure she went out the door all the faster.

Fear seared her roiling stomach as she clutched the icy doorknob. She gripped the edges of her coat and burrowed inside to protect herself from the punishing winds.

Waking up alone in a run-down motel with nothing but sleazy clothes, a hundred dollars and no memory had been bad enough. Now, she would surely freeze to death before she discovered her name and why she'd had blood on her hands.

Crunching her heels into the ice for traction, she

tugged on the door to Clyde's Travel Lodge. She slipped anyway, her hand whipping off the knob. The woozy sensation she hadn't been able to shake since waking threatened her balance. She grappled for the rail. Her sweaty palms bonded to the freezing metal. Or maybe it was blood residue, although she'd scrubbed and scrubbed until her hands were as raw as any Lady Macbeth pivotal moment.

Hang tough. Stay calm. She steadied her feet and breathing. There had to be a logical answer.

Only a couple more steps. She could manage that. The manager or clerk would have some record of her name, all the spark she would need to fire her memories.

She hoped.

The hundred dollars, hotel key and EpiPen on the bedside table hadn't brought any recollections. The telephone book in her room had helped some, even if the phones were out of order. At least she knew she'd awakened in the small town of Rockfish, Washington, and that she could order carryout from Marge's Diner until 9:00 p.m.

Great. Just what she needed, a blue plate special to erase what little she did remember—bloodred dress and hands.

She grasped the gold *D* initial necklace, the only thing that felt right in her whole insane morning. Inhaling a bracing breath that threatened to freeze her from the inside out, she grabbed the doorknob again and twisted. The wind ripped the door from her, banging it against the wall. She stumbled inside and slammed into a broad male chest.

"Steady there." A strong hand gripped her arm.

"Oh, excuse me." She winced, her own voice still sounding as unfamiliar to her as her face looked in a mirror.

"No harm, no foul."

The deep voice rumbled over her, jarring along her ravaged nerves.

Nausea born of panic roiled again. Had she met this man earlier? If she glanced up, would he recognize her?

She scavenged for a smile and let her gaze travel up the chest in front of her. A T-shirt with an Air Force logo peeked between the parted fabric of unbuttoned blue flannel. His left arm was in a sling, but his large neck bespoke strength that sent a fresh blast of apprehension through her.

Her gaze upward seemed never ending, taking this guy to at least a few inches over six feet. Hmm...he had a dimpled chin. She found that reassuring, and she needed reassurance more than she needed an hour in front of that roaring fireplace.

Broad cheekbones stretched just below slate-blue eyes.

Brooding eyes stared without a flicker of recognition.

His hand dropped away. "Come on inside before we heat the whole state."

"Sorry about that." She sidestepped him and studied

the breadth of his shoulders as he wrestled the door closed. Heaven help her if he wasn't trustworthy.

He pivoted to face her, scratching a hand along his close-cropped black hair. "What can I do for you, ma'am?"

That was it? All he had to say?

There went any hope of him knowing her. She wanted to pitch all her fears right at his feet, but feared she was more likely to toss her cookies.

That Air Force T-shirt seemed to hint she could trust him, but still. He worked here, so whatever connection he had to the military was over or through a friend. Maybe he was just an air show junkie, and God, her mind was rambling.

Bottom line, she was helpless to anyone who might take advantage of her.

A logical voice urged her to call the police, and she would, as soon as the phone lines were back in working order and she could unscramble her mind enough to think clearly. Meanwhile, she would follow her instincts, instincts being all she had.

Moving on to discovering what the register held. "I'm ready to check out."

"No need. You're already paid up. Just drop off the key."

She stuffed her hand in her pocket and clutched her fingers around the chilly steel beside her wad of cash and the EpiPen—not that she even knew what allergies to avoid.

If she passed the key over, she would be officially

homeless. So what if her only bed waited in a rustic motel so old it didn't even have key cards?

She stifled a hysterical laugh. She knew about key cards, yet didn't know her own name. "When's check-out time again?"

"Noon."

The ancient *Field and Stream* wall clock seemed to mock her, ticking away those last twenty-one minutes. She sifted through her muddled concentration for her next question.

His cool eyes settled on her dress. "Uh, but you can stay longer if you need to. I've got a busload of senior citizens due in, but not until this evening, if they can make it through the storm."

At least she could stay a few more hours without using her precious store of cash. "Do you mind printing out a copy of my receipt?"

"A copy?"

"For tax purposes."

"Tax purposes?" His eyes slid down her slinky red dress then up again without censure, but with obvious disbelief. "Sure. I gave one to your, uh, husband, but it's no trouble to shoot out another."

Husband. The word surged through her with an odd mixture of hope and the metallic taste of fear. Where was he? "Thanks. He lost his copy. I'm supposed to pick up another one, you know, taxes and all that."

"For your husband." Those brooding eyes shifted from her to the empty parking lot before returning.

"He should be back soon." She resisted the urge to fidget like a first-day kindergartner. "Could I see the owner?" Preferably, a much older, grandfatherly kind of guy without piercing eyes that saw too much.

"That would be me."

"Oh. Clyde?"

"Clyde was my father. He's dead. The place belongs to me and my sister now."

He didn't seem to be grieving when he mentioned his dad, so she didn't bother with condolences. "And you are?"

"Jacob Stone."

Her nerves began to unravel like a rolling ball of yarn she couldn't quite catch. "May I please have my receipt, Mr. Stone?"

"Just Jacob, ma'am." The man tucked his thumbs in his back pockets, looming over her, compelling, silent and dangerous. With a curt nod, he stepped away. "All right, then, one copy on its way."

Her shoulders slumped with a slow exhale. "Just Jacob," clerk, manager and owner of Clyde's Travel Lodge, circled behind the counter. He tapped through a few keys and set the printer into motion. The clicking sounded unnaturally harsh, echoing the only noise in the sparse room.

She fingered her necklace like a security blanket, tracing the *D* and looking around for something familiar. She must have seen this place the night before. A brown artificial leather sofa nestled beneath the picture window overlooking the parking lot. The style was up-to-date, but the cracks in the Naugahyde upholstery showed the toll of weather blasts. Three vending machines lined the paneled wall to the side with a brick fireplace directly across. A cheaply framed landscape poster labeled Mount Rainier hung over the mantel. The television and an office chair behind the registration counter rounded out the sparse decor.

Just Jacob ripped the paper free from the printer. It was all she could do not to jump out of her skin.

"Here you go."

"Thank you." She forced herself to take it from him slowly, casually. Their hands paused, side by side. Hers seemed so small and vulnerable beside his larger, roughened one. The paper rattled in her trembling grasp as she took it from him.

Mr. and Mrs. J. Smith. Her right hand clenched over her bare ring finger. Damn. The guy she must have trysted with hadn't even been original. Tears burned her eyes, then turned icy on her still-chilled skin.

She spun away, paper crumpled in her grip. Not even sure where she was going, only knowing she had to run, she charged out the door. The snowstorm swirled a thick white bubble around the parking lot. She couldn't see a thing past the line of tiny motel units.

Total isolation.

Her head hurt. Her whole body hurt. God, her brain was so fogged she couldn't think, much less make decisions while she waited to call the police. She sagged against the railing, mindless of the damp cold seeping through her clothes as she stared out at nothing. A nothingness vast as the void in her mind.

And the only one who could help her fill it was a man with shadows in his eyes that sent fresh shivers along her freezing skin.

Chapter 2

More contradictions. Jacob watched the woman stumble back into the hazy storm. She leaned her body weight into dragging the door closed.

Once he'd seen those tear-filled eyes, he expected a sob story and an eyelash-fluttering plea for help. Instead she'd braced her spine so rigidly, even the fifty-mile-an-hour gusts outside couldn't have knocked her over. Prideful without question.

The clothes relayed one image, her frail body another, and that haughty Midwestern voice, yet another. His gaze traveled over the woman. Around thirty, medium height. Whispery brown hair trailed her, riding the wind and revealing delicate cheekbones to match those dainty wrists and ankles. Her fresh, heart-shaped face might as well have *home fires* and *bridge club* tattooed across her forehead. He could almost smell the cookies baking through the plate-glass window.

She wouldn't be making cookies anytime soon if she froze to death wearing that neon number.

Who the hell was she? And why did he care?

So her scum boyfriend had ditched her in a hotel, leaving her stranded. It wasn't Jacob's problem. She hadn't even asked for his help. He'd helped her anyway by extending her checkout time until the phones were working again and she could call a friend to pick her up. Problem solved.

Jacob reached for his remote and began easing himself into his chair, which offered him a too-perfect view of the woman collapsing on the top step.

He'd already started toward the door when she jerked upright. She gripped the railing and began heaving onto the snowbank beside her.

Aw, hell. Jacob shrugged out of his sling and into a coat with a wince, grabbing an extra jacket for her. He wrenched open the door. Cold air in front and warmed air on his back vise-locked him until he jerked the door closed. He lowered himself beside her and waited.

Slowly she straightened and grappled in her pocket, pulling free a tissue.

He draped the extra coat over her stockinged legs. "You okay?"

She nodded, dabbing the wadded Kleenex along her

mouth like his grandma used to do after a cup of tea. "Thank you. I'll be all right in a minute."

Jacob stared down the endless length of the two-lane highway. A familiar truck droned closer, a plow wedge on front. Just like any other day here. Except for the woman beside him. "I'm not so sure I agree. Seems like you have a problem Ms....What was your name again?"

Her fingers fluttered to her necklace, the *D* glinting. She frowned. Her face cleared as her hand fell to her lap. "Dee. Dee Smith."

"Smith, huh?"

"Yes, Smith."

Let her keep her little secrets. Maybe she didn't want her indiscretion to become public knowledge. "I don't mean to pry, but it's fairly obvious you're stranded. Is there someone I can call to give you a ride?"

"There's no one."

That stunk. He remembered the feeling from when he was a kid with a dad who didn't give a crap. Now he had people he could call on 24/7 anywhere, anytime. He could give a shout out to any of his Air Force friends stationed back at Charleston Air Force base in South Carolina. He even had some closer who'd transferred to the C-17 base in Tacoma.

He didn't take that sense of family for granted, not for one second.

Dee slid her hands under the coat. "If you really meant it about staying in the room another few hours, I'll just rest, then call a cab when the phones are up and working."

"No cab's going to come from Tacoma to this microdot on the map, especially not in this weather. It's dicey if the roads will even stay open much longer."

What would she do now to dodge telling him her real story? Playing mind games with each other could be fun, if she didn't have that bleak expression plastered across her face.

He sat beside her and waited. He was patient and thrived on puzzles, like putting the pieces together in an engine so things worked right again. Restoring order, even to a car, had given him a sense of control as a teen stuck in a chaotic home.

The rust-rimmed truck on the highway slowed and swerved into the parking lot. It bounced along the rutted ice, plowing with methodical sweeps. His ear tuned to listen for any warning noises from the engine, but the hum sounded a helluva lot better now thanks to his tune-up last weekend. Installing the new battery one-handed had been a challenge, but he'd enjoyed the familiar scents, routine, being able to fix something in his hay-wire world. Apparently not much had changed since he'd left.

Dee pointed to the teenage driver. "What about her?"

With each quick turn of the Ford 250, the girl's ponytail bobbed just above her parka.

"That's my sister." Who shouldn't be out in this storm, and certainly not with her baby in tow. But Emily had run wild on her own for years. Their father had been long on smiles, jokes and unkept promises, but short on maturity, structure and follow-through. He didn't give a damn what his kids did so long as they didn't make any demands on him.

Guilt kicked at Jacob all over again for not taking Emily along when he'd left. But the state wouldn't pull her out of her father's care to stay with a military brother who was deployed most of every year. His job hadn't changed, and he needed to figure out some way for a seventeen-year-old unwed mother to care for herself and her baby. "She uses our dad's old truck to clear driveways and side roads before school for extra money. School's canceled and she shouldn't even be out at all. No help for you there, I'm afraid."

He needed to move this woman along and have a talk with his sister. Emily avoided discussing the future as if somehow that would make their problems disappear.

"Oh." Dee's blue lip quivered as Emily's truck disappeared around the office to clear the back lot.

As much as he needed to move on, he couldn't just walk away, not when tears hovered on the edges of her eyelids. "Hey, now, are you okay?"

"I'm not crying." She sniffled.

"Right. Of course you're not."

"I'm not!" The starch layered back into her voice and spine.

"Okay!" His hands raised in surrender.

Icy sludge from the plow gathered and slapped to the

side. Dee drew her feet in, tucking Jacob's coat around her ankles. Trim, delicate ankles, like the rest of her.

A slow burn started inside him.

She was prettier up close than he'd originally thought, not that he planned to do a thing about it beyond admiring the view. "I can give you a ride when the storm passes, but you're probably stuck here for at least another night until the roads clear."

Her eyes fluttered closed. "How much are the rates?"

"If you need a loan—"

"No handouts. But thank you."

He wanted to tell her pride had a way of biting folks when they least expected it. He'd been so busy flying around the world to save people in other countries he'd let down his own sister. "I can give you a ride into town later." He held up a freezing finger to stop her. "Just think it over and get back to me."

Why was he so hell-bent on settling this woman's problems? He had enough responsibility in that truck. Let the mystery woman snag a nap and come to her senses. She would either find someone to help her or accept his offer for a ride. No sweat either way.

Jacob pushed to his feet. He had better things to do than freeze his butt off for someone he didn't even know.

But first, he would shovel the walkway one more time. Just to wait for his sister to finish so he could help with her baby daughter. Right?

Damn.

He kicked through the snow and yanked free the

shovel embedded in a four-foot drift. Ouch. Just what his healing arm needed. The gunshot wound was six weeks old, the fractured bone about healed, but the incision from surgery still pulled like hell.

His muttered curses filled the air with puffy clouds. Jacob scooped a trail along the walk and flung it to the side, burying the spot where she'd thrown up. He kept shoveling, losing himself in the mundane task.

Dee didn't move. The wind kept howling down from the mountains.

Jacob shoveled past her and stopped, resting his arms on the handle. "How bad are things?"

"The worst." She dabbed her face with the tissue again, grandma-style.

He believed her. Hell, he'd been there in this very same place. Which made him wonder where she was from. Somewhere close by? He tried to recall what state the Suburban plates had sported, but he couldn't remember having read what Mr. Smith wrote on the check-in form. He'd only made sure all the boxes were filled out. Regardless of how close or far away she lived, how damn sad to be this alone.

Jacob let the icy air clear away the bitterness. He couldn't be like his old man and turn a blind eye to other people's needs.

"I have a job open here to tide you over for a few days. Doesn't pay much, but you can have a room to sleep in and all the Continental breakfast doughnuts you can eat until you figure out what to do."

She opened her mouth. "But—"

"Wait before you answer. The job's nothing glamorous. You'll be cleaning rooms. It's dirty, hard work, even when there are only a few rooms filled. You'll earn every penny I pay you."

Her lips pressed tightly together before she blurted, "There's something you should know."

More secrets? More obligation. Not a chance. "Hold on. I don't need your life story or anything."

She laughed, a high-pitched, nervous sort of sound. "Don't worry. I'm not likely to spill it anytime soon."

"Are you in trouble with the law?"

She twisted her wind-raw hands together. "Not that I know of. But I may not be around long."

"To be fair, this motel might not be around much longer, either." Selling the place—if he could even find a buyer—was an option, if he could persuade his sister to leave. "Let's just get through this next batch of tourists." He leaned forward on the shovel handle. "And no drugs."

Her nose tipped with an air a mite too haughty for a woman in her position. "Of course not."

Yet, again, he believed her, with not even one good reason to call upon, and a thousand bad ones telling him she was trouble. "Then that's all I need to know for now. About the job?"

"I'll take it. Thank you." Her eyes met his, lit with hope and gratitude.

Her pretty face shone with a gentle beauty that threatened to draw the air from his lungs more effectively than the biting wind. What the hell had he just done?

Lord, she hoped fate would cut her a break. Dee wrapped the coat tighter around her legs and considered her options.

Jacob Stone's offer had seemed the perfect answer, but "Mr. Smith's" fake registration and apparent desertion led her to believe her instincts on men hadn't been stellar even when she'd possessed a full set of memories to draw upon. God, she was so scared.

What kind of person was she? Someone who stayed in cheap motels with men who slipped away the next morning? She tried to wrap her mind around that image of herself, and it didn't fit.

Did amnesia change a person's basic nature? Perhaps.

Hopefully the phone lines would be up soon. She could put in a call to the cops, even if the roads were impassable. Maybe she had a big, fat account full of money somewhere and could spend her hundred dollars without concern while she waited.

Except that didn't feel right, either. Just as she knew she wasn't the one-night-stand kind of woman, she also knew she needed to cling to every penny of that hundred dollars.

Taking the job was the best solution for now. Having a plan didn't stop the fear, but at least her hands stopped shaking.

Dee draped Jacob's extra coat over her arm and struggled to her feet, hoping her wooziness had fled for good. The mere thought of ammonia made her want to gag. "Okay, Mr. Stone. Point me to the mop and bucket so I can get to work."

"It's Jacob. And you should change first." His gaze lingered a second too long on her dress.

She yanked her coat closed, unsure if she should bristle at his order. The guy did have a way of taking charge. She reminded herself not to be a temperamental ingrate. "Which rooms should I start with?"

He leaned on his shovel as if trying to decide whether to push the clothing issue further. Blowing snow hovered around his booted feet as he shifted his gaze to the truck sweeping through the parking lot. He stuffed the shovel into a drift. "Come on inside, and I'll get you set up."

Dee started up the steps. "How many rooms will you need cleaned if the tour bus shows?"

When he didn't answer, she pivoted at the door. Jacob knelt at the base of the porch, scooping his fingers through snow. How odd. But she didn't dare rush him.

Jacob shaped the handful and arced his arm back. He let the snowball fly, nailing the truck's hood. The Ford kept rumbling forward. He packed together a second missile and thudded the back window. The truck stopped.

The driver's-side window rolled down and a teenage face poked out, a face with a hefty addiction to eyeliner. "Yeah, bro? Did I miss someplace?"

"Park it, Emily. School's canceled. Build a snow-man or something." He blew into his cupped hands, wincing as he moved the arm that had been in a sling earlier.

"I'm almost through here." Wind streaked her wheat-blond ponytail, revealing the crimson strip dyed through.

"You're done now."

"Sure, Jacob. Whatever." She rolled up the window, kicked the truck in gear and proceeded to plow the next row.

Jacob lobbed another snowball into the retreating truck bed. "Damn fool girl."

"Her or me?" Dee couldn't resist mumbling.

He either didn't hear or chose to ignore the comment. Jacob stomped his feet as he turned. "Let's get your supplies. Only one room needs cleaning. We can test you on that. The rest only need light touch-ups, some dusting and airing."

As they walked inside, he rambled off a list of tasks. She registered his clipped phrases, all the while absorbing details around her to fill the terrifying emptiness within. She glanced at the framed buffalo prints over the fireplace. A faded map of Washington spread above a brochure rack. The scary ache didn't even begin to fade.

Jacob Stone was the only person she could remember speaking to since waking, a strangely quiet man who took in stray amnesiacs and worried about his teenage sister on the road.

He and that young girl were the only people she'd seen face-to-face. Years of experiences with others had been lost, shrouded by an impenetrable fog. It was enough to make a person crazy.

If she wasn't already.

He stared through his windshield at the lodge with *her* inside.

She'd been in and out of sight most of the morning. He couldn't take his eyes off the shape of her, especially when the wind plastered her clothes into a tighter fit like now as she ducked into another room. Heat from the vents didn't come close to the temperature pumping through him.

Want and hate, both hot, pumped through him.

Women screwed up everything. They always wanted more, more, more from a guy. She was just like the rest in the end. *She* was the messed up one, not him.

So what if he watched her through binoculars while parked on a side road? That didn't make him a perv since she belonged to him anyway. Yeah, she still fascinated him even though he'd already had her.

He hated that about her, the way she had a hold over him. There were times he thought he would do anything to get rid of her. Then she drew him in again with her smile, her laugh, her touch.

Claustrophobia filled the vehicle in gusts as thick as the exhaust puffing from the tailpipe. He should just go. Somebody might see him lurking around. He could come up with an excuse, but it would seem weird. More than ever he needed to appear blameless.

Things would look bad enough when he got rid of her for good.

Chapter 3

Dee attacked the tub with a rag.

Surely routine household chores should stir a memory. How many tubs had she scrubbed over the years? One too many as of today since Jacob had underestimated the number of dirty rooms. Did his regular maid have bad eyesight?

Jacob Stone had been right about one thing. Cleaning was dirty, hard work. And she thanked God for the job plus the monotonous distraction it provided.

She'd done more than dust and air the extra rooms, but she felt obligated. Jacob would have been well within his rights to toss her into a snowbank. Of course with any luck, someone would come looking for her soon, whisk her off to a hot meal and soft bed, a bed she hadn't made.

Meanwhile, she would pay her way while she waited to reclaim her identity. Her pride demanded it. Pride? The notion seemed misplaced given her current mess, but she didn't have much else left.

Dee slumped against the bathroom wall and clutched her legs to her chest. What had robbed her of her past? She'd scoured every inch of her head, and there wasn't a telling lump to be found, just a sore spot that could have come from brushing her hair too hard.

Could she trust someone on the tour bus to help her? Possibly, but not worth betting the bank. That just left her new boss.

What a puzzling man. Not that she had much to compare him to. He seemed determined to help her when he had absolutely no obligation.

Around midday, he'd slipped through the door, set a plate of food on the table and silently lumbered back out before she could speak. While she hadn't been able to tolerate more than a mouthful of the sandwich, she'd stared out the window at his footprints long after he'd been swallowed by the circling snow. His thoughtfulness had filled her with a sense of security far more nourishing than two slices of bread and some turkey.

Dee stretched her legs the length of the minuscule bathroom. Every muscle resisted, tightening, urging her to curl up and sleep.

Not a chance. She had to break out the vacuum and

get back to work before her boss caught her napping on the job.

She flung the can of scrubbing bubbles into the supply bucket just as voices swelled from the next room. Dee conquered her aching muscles and stood, ducking her head out the bathroom door. "Hello? Who's there?"

The television blared to life from the stand. She stepped into the room and found the girl from the plow truck—Emily, Jacob's sister—pitching aside the remote control.

"Hi, there." Emily sat cross-legged in the middle of one of the unmade beds, a jelly-filled doughnut in one hand, foam cup of milk in the other resting on her knee. On the television, a game show contestant puzzled over an answer that could win her a Winnebago and a year's supply of beef jerky.

All of that faded for Dee as her gaze focused on the sleeping baby in the middle of the bed. Swaddled in a pink sleeper with footies, the infant appeared to be no more than two or three months old.

Jacob had a child and recruited his sister for baby-sitting? She'd just assumed from his bare ring finger that he was single.

Dee notched down the volume with the remote. "I would tell you to make yourself comfortable, but—"

"I figured you wouldn't mind some company while you worked. I'm Emily. Emily Stone." She patted the sleeping baby on her little round belly. "This is Madison."

Still no clue who the infant belonged to and Dee didn't bother asking. Her overtaxed brain seemed to do better by assimilating information as it came to her.

Emily appeared to be settling in for a long stay, and Dee wasn't sure she had enough energy for the mental gymnastics needed to dodge more questions. "Weren't you going to build a snowman?"

Emily tore her doughnut open. "Like I can wait another minute without the inside skinny on you."

"There's nothing to know." What an understatement.

"Yeah, right. I figure I'll just hang out. Madison's gotta eat soon anyway." Emily sipped her milk. Her curious eyes peered over the rim.

Dee eyed the cup, her stomach simultaneously growling and rolling. Best to stay away from food. She took in the girl's Army fatigue pants and tight white T-shirt, hair-thin silver chains floating along her collarbone.

"So?" Emily licked away her milk mustache.

The girl wasn't going to leave without something. The truth, or as close as she could guess, seemed a safe bet.

"My boyfriend skipped out on me." Dee spritzed the mirror with Windex and began wiping.

"That bites. Guess I'm really lucky to have Chase." The baby whimpered and Emily lifted her like a pro.

Then she hiked up her T-shirt and latched the baby onto her breast.

Dee blinked, surprised. Well, that solved one mystery, and brought an unwelcome swell of relief that the baby was Jacob's niece.

Emily frowned, her hand cupping Madison's head as the baby nursed. "I didn't think to ask. Do you mind my nursing her in front of you?"

Dee shook off her distracting thoughts. "No. Of course not. We all have to eat, right?"

Emily's face smoothed into a smile. "You're cool. Good." The sheets rustled. A small slurp sounded, before Emily continued, "Okay, so your guy blew out. How did you end up with a bottle of Windex and a broom?"

"I'm helping out to pay my bill until the storm passes."

Emily set her cup on the end table. "Must have been some party last night."

At least she could answer that one honestly. "I don't remember."

"That *really* bites." Sticking her finger into the center of her doughnut, she scooped out the filling. She sucked it clean and flung the rest of the pastry in the trash can. "Do you think my brother's hot?"

Dee's hand froze on the mirror. "Pardon?"

"Hot. A real hottie. Good-looking. Well, for an old guy, anyway."

How old am I? The question blindsided her. When would she get used to questioning the most elementary things about herself and coming up empty? Hopefully she wouldn't have to.

So how old was she? Emily seemed a child. Jacob Stone looked to be around thirty and felt like a contemporary. Dee decided that put her somewhere in her early thirties, as well.

She swiped along the edges of the mirror. No one could call Jacob anything but virile. "He's not exactly ancient."

Emily grinned smugly before continuing. "He doesn't live here in this dump, in case you were wondering. He's in the Air Force, stationed in South Carolina. He's an in-flight mechanic for one of the big cargo planes," she said with unmistakable pride as she shifted the baby to the other side to feed. "He's served a lot of time in the Middle East. He even got hurt on a mission last Christmas."

His broad chest in that T-shirt came to mind, along with the sling he'd first worn. "That must have been scary for you."

The teen stared down at her baby's head and smoothed a hand over the fine blond hair. "It's been a tough couple of months, with having Madison, then Jacob getting hurt and Dad dying."

Dee ached to hug the young girl carrying so many adult problems at once. She started to move toward her when Emily tossed back her head with a smile and stand-off bravado. "So, do you think Jacob is hot?"

"Not meaning to be rude, but I just met the guy and I'm not in any position for a relationship right now." She wasn't up to matching wits with the ponytail contingent. "Um, I really need to make that bed."

"Sure, no problem." Emily secured the baby in the cradle of her arms and moved to a chair. "I didn't mean to get in the way. I just don't get as much time to talk to people as I used to."

Those simply spoken words without even a hint of self-pity tugged at Dee more than if the girl had poured out buckets of tears. She understood too well the fear from losing control of her world.

"I appreciate the company." Dee scooped off the musty spread and whipped a fresh one into a fluttering parachute over the bed. "Want to tell me about your boy-friend?"

"His name's Chase. He's, like, so hot," she said, her dialect an odd mix of Generation Y meets farm town as she listed his every "awesome" attribute.

Dee clutched the top sheet to her chest. Generation Y. How could she recall such catchphrases but not her own name? She swallowed down a fresh well of nausea and searched for why she'd hooked on the phrase.

Nothing.

She remembered about key cards and movies, but no real life experiences to accompany the information. She sagged to the edge of the bed.

"You okay?" Emily asked.

Dee jerked. "Huh? Oh, yes, I'm fine. I'm a little dis-tracted today." She swallowed hard and searched for normal conversation. "So, uh, is Chase Madison's father?"

Emily nodded, thankfully not offended by the ques-tion. She hitched the baby on her shoulder and tugged her shirt back in place. "We're gonna get married when we're older."

A tap sounded from the door just before it opened. A blast of air funneled into the room as Jacob stepped inside, his broad shoulders momentarily sealing the entry.

His height no longer intimidating, her nerves smoothed as if an iron had flattened all the disruptive wrinkles. How did he do that? Manage to calm her world with a job offer and a sandwich?

Jacob slammed the door closed behind him. He swiped the baby from Emily's shoulder and lowered his oversize body into the seat to finish burping the infant. "Hey, there, runt. How many doughnuts did your mama pilfer?"

"Only one, that you know of." Emily grinned without a flicker of remorse. "Madison needs the fruit in that raspberry pastry."

"Quit eating up the profits."

"Deduct it from my portion of the inheritance from Dad."

"Yeah, yeah," he grumbled, his face creasing into an almost-smile.

The conversation hummed on, but Dee couldn't focus on anything except the tableau of that tiny baby held so securely in oversize hands.

Her breath hitched. Emily was right. Jacob Stone was hot. A glance at those trim hips and long legs encased in overwashed denim sent a liquid heat flooding through Dee that rivaled any sugar jolt from a raspberry tart.

What kind of woman did that make her? Did she get

warm and soft feelings over every man who crossed her path? She didn't like that image of herself. Could she simply be drawn to Jacob because he'd been the one to toss her a lifeline?

Emily grabbed her coat off the back of the chair and reached for her daughter. "I'm outta here. You old folks reek of gloom and doom."

Jacob propped a boot on the edge of the bed, blocking Emily's escape. "Where're you going? The weather's not showing any signs of letting up."

"Just to Chase's." Emily draped a thick yellow blanket over the baby. "Don't say no or I'll just sneak out. You're my brother, not my father, and even he didn't rag on me every time I wanted to go somewhere."

He slid his foot to the ground. "Take the truck and be careful."

"Sure, Gramps. I'll even call you on your cell if I can pick up any reception in this weather." She jerked a thumb over her shoulder. "And get this lady into some warmer clothes and shoes before she, like, loses a toe to frostbite. Of course, if she wears anything of yours, she'll be a fugitive from the fashion police."

Police. Dee's throat closed with a new thought. What if the police were after her? She couldn't imagine herself as a criminal. But she wouldn't have imagined she'd choose a low-cut silk dress if she couldn't see the proof glaring back at her from the mirror.

And she didn't even want to think about what the hundred on the bedside table had meant.

Jacob tipped back his chair. "Thanks for the fashion commentary, kid. You're one to talk."

"Truth hurts." Emily tossed her ponytail over her shoulder, red streak glinting. "Later, dudes."

"Don't forget to call," he shouted after the closing door.

Emily had just assumed he would loan Dee clothes, no question or hesitation. She had to admit, he did have a way of taking charge and reordering her world with seeming ease.

Jacob swung his feet up to occupy the vacated chair. Chilly silvery-blue eyes whispered over her. "I imagine you're not staying in that dress because it's your favorite. No suitcase?"

Dee backed a step as if that might distance her from the impact of that shivery gaze. She wasn't even sure whom to trust. Keep focused. *Cell phone.* He had a cell phone. She should have thought to ask about one earlier. Now she could call for help and find her family—or perhaps end up in jail. "Uh, no. I don't have a change of clothes."

He gripped the chair arms and shoved to his feet. "Meet me over at the office when you finish up here."

"Sure. About ten more minutes." She tucked the spread along the pillows, taking more time to even the edges than she needed until he left.

Ten minutes and she could try for a cell phone connection. Regardless of the outcome, she wanted to know. All she needed to do was ask him for the phone.

Was she ready for what she might find?

* * *

Jacob refilled the coffeemaker in the lobby while he waited for Dee to finish her call. Apparently she'd thought of a friend to contact after all.

At least she'd cleaned the rooms before cutting out. He would be ready if the bus managed to make it through the storm, and the regular maid would be over her bout of flu soon.

Dee's muffled words wafted from the other room. He settled in the creaky leather chair behind the check-in desk and let her soothing tones flow over him. She had a nice voice, gentle and soft like a wind whispering over airplane wings. If only she weren't shoveling lies his way faster than a snowplow.

Her voice quieted. Jacob tugged open a file drawer and tried not to watch the sway of her hips as she glided down the hall connecting his rooms to the reception area.

Dee paused in the doorway, her shoulder resting against the frame. She clutched the phone to her chest. "Thanks. The connection was crackly, but I got through."

"You're all set then."

"No."

So much for a return to peace. "Your ride can't make it out here yet?"

She shook her head. Her grip tightened around the cell phone until one of the buttons chirped. "Is the job open long-term? Well, as long as you plan to keep this place open. I may need it for a while."

"I've already got someone who comes in to clean." Her panicked eyes compelled him to add, "But Grace's arthritis is acting up, and she could use the extra help."

Which was the truth, except now he had two house-keeping employees and a floundering business. Great. He would bankrupt the place at a time he needed to secure a future for his sister.

"Thanks again for letting me use the phone." She leaned to place it on the counter. Her dress gaped open, giving a full view of creamy breasts encased in lace.

Jacob shifted his gaze to a file, not nearly as inter-esting but a hell of a lot less tempting. "Let's get you into something warmer."

The now predictable battle waged in her eyes, pride versus practicality. She glanced down at that slinky little dress and nibbled her lip, then her spine straight-ened to a debutante stance that matched her face far more than the clothes. He could see pride had won.

Dee clasped the neckline closed. "Thank you, but you've done enough already."

"I'm not offering to let you raid my closet. Emily's right about my wardrobe—or lack of one." Since he wore a flight suit most of the time, he didn't need much in the way of civilian clothes. He gestured for her to follow him to the hall that connected the front office to the living quarters. "There's a lost-and-found box of un-claimed items folks have left in the rooms. You can help yourself."

She scrunched her toes in her shoes and looked out

the ice-laced window. Starch leaked from her spine. "If you're sure it's all right. Consider it trade for the cleaning I've done today. No handouts."

"Haven't you ever heard about the joy of giving? Consider it an early Valentine's Day gift." Only a week away. Did she have someone besides Mr. Smith out there? Shaking off the thought, Jacob swung open the supply-closet door. "Rifle through and take anything you need. You can scrub a few extra sinks if it'll make you feel better."

Her thin shoulders slumped before she pivoted to face him. She reached, her trembling fingers hesitating an inch shy of touching him. "I don't mean to sound ungrateful."

The heat of her hand crackled through the air and scorched his chest. An image of lace burned an imprint in his mind. His thoughts twisted along paths he had no business traveling, paths that led to wrapping his body up with her, even if only for a mind-numbingly short time.

He should swaddle her in a few layers of clothes and march her out the door for more reasons than he'd originally thought. "You're welcome."

Jacob lost himself in the routine of paperwork. For all of four minutes. Maybe he should shovel more snow one-handed—ouch. Heaven knew that could keep him busy and cool him off. Or was there enough snow in a Washington winter for that just now?

He tipped his chair for a better view into the hall and

let himself study her for an unrestrained moment. She'd made a small pile of clothes to use, a larger pile of obvious discards neatly folded to the other side.

She glanced over her shoulder. "Did Emily get to her boyfriend's house okay?"

Jacob thudded his chair to the ground along with his thoughts, better all the way around. "Uh-huh."

She hooked an arm over the rim of the box, her slim legs tucked to the side. "Am I bothering you?"

Yeah. "No. Why?"

"I was only trying to make polite conversation, fill the silence a little. We're stuck here together, after all. I didn't mean to be a pest. Just say the word if you don't want to talk."

"Didn't mean to be rude. I'm buried in paperwork." There. That sounded like a polite excuse.

"Sorry."

He scrolled down the computer screen and began cross-referencing expenditures for tax returns. His father hadn't been much for bookkeeping. Jacob just prayed the old man had actually paid his taxes.

He needed to come up with enough money to get Emily through the college years. His pay didn't come close to covering that. Plus, even if he could convince her to move in with him, she would need child care during school hours and someone to stay with her when he was deployed.

Dee cleared her throat and coughed, still dainty sounds. "Little Madison is precious. And the baby's father seems…involved? It was nice of you to let them have time together today."

Jacob slipped in a backup CD. "Like I had a choice. As Emily said, I'm her brother not her father."

Pain flashed in Dee's eyes before they turned flat as a slap of mud on a windshield. He'd been curt, but the whole situation frustrated him. He wanted to beat the crap out of Chase, but Emily insisted she loved him and they were going to get married. The situation made his blood boil, so he was better off staying quiet.

The rustling of clothes brought his attention back to the present as Dee sorted through the box. How could one small woman explode into his life so fully in the span of a few hours?

"I have big feet!"

"What?" Jacob pivoted in his chair, doing a slow take toward her.

Dee sat in the middle of the discarded pile. A tennis shoe dangled off the end of her toes like Cinderella's stepsisters trying on the glass slipper.

She snatched the shoe off her foot. "Did I say that out loud? Sorry, but my feet are kind of big."

"You're only just noticing?" This was the strangest woman he'd ever met.

"I, uh, just forget sometimes that the rest of the world doesn't have snow skis for feet."

If he didn't get her outfitted soon, she would never return to her room. He gave up the fight and moved to help her. He tucked into the closet and pulled out another box.

Jacob knelt beside it. Beside her. Damn, but he'd gone from putting distance between them to landing himself six inches away. "Dig deep. There's a pair of gym shoes near the bottom that might come closer to fitting."

Dee peered inside, keeping a white-knuckled grip on the vee neck of her dress. It didn't make one bit of difference. Funny thing about the male imagination, he didn't actually have to see what was beneath that dress to have a clear mental picture.

He buried his hands in the box, rummaging around until he found the near-new Nikes. Jacob tossed them onto her pile. He also grabbed a ski sweater, a long one, and added it to her stack, as well. "You can go shopping with your first paycheck. Which reminds me. If you're going to work here long-term, you'll need to fill out one of these."

Jacob lumbered to his feet, knees and ankles popping as he stood. He shuffled through a stack of papers on his desk and passed one to her.

"What's this?"

"Your W-2 form."

"W-2?" Dee's face turned whiter than the snow in the parking lot, her wide brown eyes the only splash of color.

"Yeah. Just fill in your name and address. I'll take care of the rest when I file it. You know. For next year's taxes."

Dee sagged to the edge of her bed. She wanted to crawl beneath the covers and never come out. The Tacoma Police Department hadn't told her anything useful on the phone, instead insisting she needed to come in once the highway cleared. They'd relayed only enough to let her know she didn't fit the descriptions from any missing persons' reports.

She clutched her little wad of clothes closer, bringing to mind an image of Emily cradling Madison earlier. Dee pressed her small bundle to her belly and rocked. Tears begging for release clogged her chapped nose. Still she rocked, refusing to cry. If she started, the fear would win. Just like if she crawled under those covers she might never tunnel back out.

At least she had a home, four paneled walls with her choice of two beds. Hers sported red plaid comforters to go with the shiny veneer furniture and cheap water-color of Puget Sound. Yes, she had a home. For now.

The W-2 form glared at her from beside the TV where she'd tossed it. How would she talk her way around this one? She wouldn't, not in a shimmery crimson dress and do-me-sailor pumps.

Dee unrolled her bundle of clothes like some hobo's pack. Two pairs of sweatpants. A couple of T-shirts. An overlong sweater. And tennis shoes. She'd relented and let Jacob toss in three pairs of his socks.

She peeled off the dress and panty hose with great relish. Forget practicality. She flung both into the trash. Without question, that can would be emptied pronto by the Lodge's newest housekeeping employee.

As she stood in her lace bra and panties, Dee realized her body looked no more familiar than her face. How surreal to become reacquainted with herself at thirty-some-odd years old.

She extended her arms, twisting the right to one side and then the other arm. She discovered a faded, inch-long scar just below her left elbow and paused to trace it with her finger.

What else didn't she know about herself?

On impulse, she tugged off her bra and checked the tag: 34B. Not overly endowed, but enough to catch the attention of a certain sexy-eyed man.

She shrugged back into the bra and told herself to quit losing focus. Who she'd been didn't matter as much as who she became from this point forward. She wouldn't repeat her "Mr. Smith" mistake by turning weak-kneed over the first hunk to cross her path.

Dee whipped a T-shirt over her head and stepped into sweatpants, wriggling them over her hips. Her hands paused midtug. She couldn't have seen what she thought she had, could she? She eased the sweats down a notch.

She stared at the map of stretch marks scrolled across her stomach.

"Oh my God." She blinked and looked again.

Nausea kicked into overdrive. Her hands twitched away. The pants snapped back, covering what she wasn't ready to view.

"Calm down," she muttered, not even caring that she was talking to herself since she'd decided she might well be crazy anyway. "Stretch marks can come about any number of ways. Maybe I'm a diet junkie with a ballooning weight problem. I've just got babies on the brain because of little Madison."

Slowly she inched the pants lower, following the milky-white ladders all the way to—

A scar. A bikini-cut, puckered scar. Just like a Cesarean section scar.

Her legs turned to soup. Dee folded into a heap on the floor. All the bottled tears and terror gushed free. Fists pressed to her stomach, she scavenged for control, strength, reason in a world turned inside out.

Her time to plan had ended. If she had a child out there somewhere, she had to find her or him. Fast.

And that meant trusting Jacob Stone with everything and pray he wasn't another "Mr. Smith."

Chapter 4

Jacob pushed away from the computer. The numbers weren't going to change anytime soon and the busload of seniors should be arriving any minute now. At least he could accommodate them.

Whatever Dee's secrets, she made one hell of a great worker. She'd accomplished more in a day than most would in a week. He'd found nothing wrong with any of her rooms. Not at all what he'd expected from a party girl.

More than her face didn't fit the profile some of her initial behavior indicated. She could have cried or pleaded her way into an extension on her room, and most men would have caved. Dee hadn't even tried.

She'd shown a lot of grit on a day that would have taken most folks down. He admired that. Emily liked her, too.

He sat upright.

Could Dee be the answer to his problems? An idea started to form in his mind. She seemed to be down on her luck, with no one to call. Maybe she wouldn't mind relocating.

He'd already begun working on a transfer to McChord Air Force Base in Tacoma. He qualified for a family humanitarian transfer, given he was his sister's guardian—Madison's, too. Emily didn't want to move even an hour away from Chase, and Jacob would still be gone too long and often for the teen to be alone out here, especially with a baby.

He wouldn't trust a stranger with his sister, but getting to know more about Dee certainly had merit.

Through the window, he saw her step from her room, the halogen lights casting a domelike effect over the snow-covered parking lot. The Cascade Mountain Range loomed dimly in the distance. Her brisk strides carried her across concrete, snowflakes sprinkling down around her. At least she wasn't shivering this time, just moving with efficiency in her new-used gray sweatpants. Somehow she made even grungy workout clothes look elegantly sexy.

No sex thoughts, dude. He needed to get his mind back on the plan. Find out more about Dee Smith. His life had been fraying at the seams for long enough.

Time to start pulling things back together, starting tonight with Dee.

She pushed inside, her nose pink from the cold.

He stood to help her close the door, catching a whiff of her clean hair, which only made him itch to test the feel of it between his fingers. "Nice pants."

"Huh?" She glanced down and plucked at the loose cotton. "Oh, they're definitely warmer. Thank you."

Dee slipped out of her coat. Her freshly washed hair crackled into a static halo. The coal-black sweater left her face paler than before, and he worried she'd worked too hard. Were her eyes red rimmed from tears or the elements?

Either way, she needed him as much as he needed her at the moment. He just had to decide how to approach her in a way that wouldn't leave her feeling pressured about her job.

Five minutes ago, he would have laughed at the thought of asking Dee to walk across the street with him. Now, he warmed to the idea of getting to know her better—for his sister's benefit. "Have you had anything to eat since lunch?"

She dropped the W-2 form onto the check-in counter. "Never mind about food. We need to talk."

Dee sat at the kitchenette table in Jacob's back-room apartment. She flattened her palms against the scarred oak surface, the only way to keep them from shaking. Forget trying to drink the can of Coke waiting in front of her.

She had scrounged the courage to talk to him, only to have the telephone repair crew put in their appearance. Jacob had asked her to wait in his apartment since he wanted to talk to her, too. She would bet good money his topic would be less upsetting.

The barnlike room echoed with silence. Located off the Lodge's lobby, it held the basics, a sofa and oversize recliner. The roof angled up over a bed across the room tucked in a loft. Her gaze skittered away and back to the living area. Given the masculine air, she imagined his father must have lived here. From her time cleaning, she now knew that Emily lived in two hotel rooms with connecting doors, located beside this apartment. Emily *and* her baby.

Dee swallowed hard. The scar on her stomach itched.

How could a mother simply cease to exist? She must have hired a babysitter if she'd planned to meet with "Mr. Smith." Or her child could be with his or her father.

Her ring finger was bare, no cheater-mark tan line in sight to show she'd worn a ring recently. While not proof positive, it reassured her somewhat.

Dee refused to believe she might be an unfaithful spouse. Regardless, she must be late with pickup or a phone call, or would be soon. Someone would report her missing.

Him or her? A son or a daughter? How awful not to know even that much. Not knowing didn't make the urge to protect any less powerful.

Of course, having a C-section scar didn't necessarily mean she'd kept the child. Maybe she'd been in a situation like Emily's and chose to give her newborn up for adoption?

Another possibility speared her. Heaven forbid, the baby might have died.

All maybes aside, she had to operate on the assumption that she did have a live child out there somewhere, and that meant enlisting Jacob's help.

His heavy tread sounded in the hall just before Jacob ducked through the doorway. "Sorry you had to wait. Phone lines are in working order again."

"Good." Nerves bubbled in her throat like a foaming soda. She'd been ready to tell him and now the words wouldn't come.

"I checked in with the dispatcher, and the tour bus is an hour away. So I have some downtime for a late supper." He opened the refrigerator and shoved aside a gallon of milk, unveiling a covered pot. "Pickings are pretty sparse around here. Good thing Emily ate with Chase's family before coming home."

He walked with ease around the minuscule kitchen, maneuvering with a lanky-limbed grace to pull out stoneware bowls, turn on the stove, place the pot on the burner. He didn't do anything quickly, but with steady purpose, opening and closing drawers as he worked. "Marge's Diner serves up good country cooking, but I don't want to leave Emily here alone to deal with all those tourists."

Jacob stirred the stew. "Rockfish isn't large, but it's a

tight-knit community. Emily will have already told Chase's mom about you, which is the same as putting an ad in the *Rockfish Weekly,* but faster since it comes with daily updates. By Sunday, you'll be the hot topic at church potlucks along with the latest Jell-O mold recipe."

Dee let him talk without interrupting. His bass tones washed over her, instilling a peace she hadn't felt since she'd awakened, peace she desperately needed now more than ever. Had she always been attracted to this sort of man? Or had her episode with Mr. Smith rattled her into an awareness of men who wore honor on their sleeves?

Or in Jacob's case, a worn Air Force T-shirt.

"We might as well preempt them with a trip to Marge's tomorrow and introduce you around. You can meet almost everyone there. The roads should open up for regular traffic by supper tomorrow." Jacob lounged a lazy hip against the counter. "What do you say?"

She stared at him until his words registered. He couldn't be asking her out to eat. Could he? The roof seemed to lower, shrinking the room. Beside Jacob Stone, everything seemed small. He probably had plenty of women bringing him Jell-O molds.

Of course he wasn't asking her out. She'd taken a long look at herself, and she didn't find the final product all that impressive. She seemed more like a regular robin with plenty of beige and brown, splashed with that garish red dress across her middle.

Dee gripped the can to quell her shaking. "Sure. I

should meet everyone and dispel rumors. I wouldn't want to ruin your reputation."

"I'm not worried about that." He rubbed a thumb along his forehead, then turned back to the counter. "First, we have to take care of food now. Is there anything you can't eat? Any allergies I should know of?"

She thought of the EpiPen she kept close. This seemed like the perfect opening. "I don't know."

Jacob glanced over his shoulder. "Excuse me?"

"I don't know if I'm allergic to anything."

"Okay." His brows met for a moment before he shrugged. "Then it's leftover stew. Any problems with that?"

"I don't know."

He pivoted on one heel to face her, a tic starting in the corner of one eye. "Don't feel obligated to stay for dinner if you're too hung over from your night out."

This wasn't going well at all. "That's not what I meant."

"Then feel free to explain what you did mean."

"That's just it. I don't know." She braced her back against the chair. "The first thing I remember is waking up here this morning."

Jacob's whole body straightened into a steely line of tension. Muscles rippled beneath his Air Force T-shirt.

Her hands clenched so tightly the aluminum can dented. The ping reverberated in the silence. If he didn't talk soon, she would snap. "Well?"

"That son of a bitch."

What? "Who?"

"Your 'Mr. Smith.'" Jacob stomped across the yellowed linoleum for two lengthy paces before kneeling at her feet. "We have to get you to a doctor, make sure you aren't having some adverse reaction to the drugs. You were sick earlier, and you're pale. You may not be over the worst." He scrubbed a restless hand over his military-short hair. "Damn it, I wonder if he used Rohypnol or GHB."

His words offered a flicker of hope. Could that be it? "Amnesia drugs?"

"Yeah, episodic amnesia meds. Creep in a bar drops one in a woman's drink. She blacks out for a while, then forgets what happened to her the night before."

Disappointment tasted more bitter than bile. "Only one night?"

"Roughly. That happened to the girlfriend of someone in my squadron about a year ago. The experience really put her through hell." He cleared his throat. "I'll get somebody in here to handle the desk while—"

"Jacob."

"—I'm gone. I'll throw the truck in four-wheel drive, and we'll—"

"Stop!"

"What?" He pressed a broad palm to her forehead. "Are you ill?"

The comfort of his touch left her on shaky ground, but she couldn't afford to weaken now. "I haven't just forgotten a few hours. I can't remember anything."

Dee lifted a trembling hand from her can and nudged

the W-2 form toward him with one finger. "I can't fill this out because I don't know my real name or address. I can't tell you anything about myself."

His gaze shifted from compassionate to suspicious. "Nothing?"

"I'm afraid not."

His eyes went from suspicious to piercing blue. Then he laughed.

"Did you hear me?"

Another laugh rolled free, a dark rumbly sound like an incoming storm. "Oh, yeah, I heard you." He shook his head. "I'm laughing at myself, not you."

"Somehow that doesn't make me feel better right now."

Jacob pulled the bubbling stew from the burner and pitched the pot holder into the sink. "You're saying you have amnesia."

"Yes, that's exactly what I'm saying."

"That's a good one." He lounged against the counter. "You've got a bump on your head. Right?"

She reached to feel around under her loose hair and yeah, the tender spot was still there. A lump, too? Or just a lumpy skull? Tough to tell, but maybe that was the cause. "As a matter of fact, I do."

"Of course." He nodded, obviously doubtful. "I would have chosen the alien abduction route. Has more flair. Maybe even toss in an Elvis sighting for fun."

Her hand drifted to her stomach, just over her scar and a churning well of panic. She'd thought through a thousand scenarios where someone might take advantage of her vulnerability, but she'd never considered she wouldn't be trusted. "I'm sorry I don't have a huge gash on my head to offer as proof. But you have to believe me."

She stuffed down a sense of steely pride and anger she could ill afford right now.

His chest rose with each steady breath. "You know, Dee Smith, there's one thing that absolutely pushes my buttons, and that's someone who lies to me."

"But I'm not—"

"Amnesia?" He nudged the form back to her. "If you want to keep your job, you'll have to come up with a better story than that."

"You don't believe me."

Jacob snorted. He'd meant what he said about hating liars. His father had backed out on promises, concocted grandiose schemes, flat out fabricated too many times. A need for truth, people he could trust, had driven Jacob to join the military.

After thirteen years in the Air Force traveling the world, he'd seen it all. But in all that time he hadn't come across a Dee Smith yet. "Do you really think I intend to pass out a pay slip without running a background check or filing paperwork?"

Apparently she did. There went the possibility of hiring her on as help with Emily.

Dee's head fell to rest on her folded hands. "Perfect end to a perfectly wretched day."

Jacob refused to let the dejected slump of her shoulders sway him. "You can always tell me the truth."

"Yeah, right." She sat up again in the dinette chair.

"If you're in some kind of trouble with the law—"

She tipped her face toward him, her defeated expression replaced by tight-lipped frustration. Or could it be anger?

"Hmm. Am I in trouble with the cops? How would I know? Aliens erased my memory in their sensory deprivation chamber. My whole history is stored on their spaceship with Elvis flying it through the galaxy at light speed."

"Now that's more like it."

Spunky as well as prideful. If only the evening had led to dinner instead of this. She'd had a bad day? In the past six weeks he'd been shot and lost his father.

"Never mind." Dee snatched her coat from the back of her chair and charged toward the door, arms pumping.

"Running away again? I'm getting mighty damned tired of chasing you out into the snow."

"Who asked you to?"

She had a point. She also had a great set of hips twitching beneath that bulky sweater and his body had picked one hell of an inconvenient time to react. "Where do you think you're going?"

"To my room." She spun to face him, her hair swinging a satiny blanket around her face. "It is still my room if I pay for it, isn't it? Even if I don't work here anymore."

"How do you plan to finance that one?"

"Elvis floated me a loan before he left." Dee stuffed her arms into her coat and marched through the archway.

Yeah, right, she'd gone to get money. She would probably hole up for the night until she could cut out or concoct a better story.

Jacob glanced at the empty chair across the room, a seat with a missing spoke on the back. He'd been thirteen, tipped the chair and fell over. His mother had been alive in those days and had given him an icepack for his sore head.

No amnesia there. In fact, too many memories floated around this place.

Jacob pulled a spoon from the drawer with half the anticipation he'd felt when starting the meal. He turned to start eating straight from the pot—and stopped.

Dee stood framed in the archway, her fists clutched by her side, her cheeks flushed from the elements.

Passing time with her wouldn't be a hardship. Except she didn't look all that happy with him. Her eyes glinted with icicles that rivaled the spikes frozen from his eaves.

Dee glided across the room like a debutante and placed folded bills on the table. "There's enough to cover tonight. No need to drive me into town tomorrow. I'll hitch a ride on the tour bus."

"So you have somewhere to go after all." He tossed his spoon on the counter. Just as he'd predicted, she would slip from his life as quickly as she stumbled into it.

"Sure."

"Well, then, I guess that's it." Jacob slid the cash

from the table and wove the folded paper through his fingers, flipping it twice. He didn't need or want her money, just the woman who'd had the patience to pass time with a mouthy teenager.

Lifting her hand, he pressed the cash into her palm. "Don't worry about the room. You earned it today. I don't think the IRS will come after me for one day's work-for-a-room trade off."

Her hand felt good in his, small and soft. Her pulse fluttered against him like a bird, her bones easily as fragile. He couldn't make himself let go.

With a twitch, she tried to pull away, then grew still, too still. Tight lines around her mouth eased. Her brown eyes shifted, melting into a warm shade of chocolate.

She swayed, ever so slightly, toward him.

Still he cradled her hand in his, his forearms so close to her breasts he could feel the heat of her. He could also smell the lingering scent of hotel cleaning supplies, but it mingled with something essentially *Dee*. Something unique, intoxicating, more unique than any of those high-priced perfumes he'd seen marketers hocking on television.

Of its own volition, his head dipped. His chin brushed just beside her temple. He filled his lungs and senses with another lingering breath of her hair, of her. *Dee*. "Just tell me your name. I can help you through whatever's going on. Running never solved anything."

Hypocrite. He forced himself not to flinch. He hadn't been around for his sister.

Dee's hand fisted in his. Easing back a step, she placed the money on the table by the salt and pepper shakers before turning on her heels.

Regret and frustration jockeyed for dominance in his testosterone-fogged brain. Why was his gut twisting into knots over this woman he'd only just met?

Pausing, she spun back and carefully peeled off three more dollars. She slapped them on the table. "Here. This should be enough to cover my call on your cell phone to the Tacoma Police Department."

Dee cleared the doorway before he could close his mouth.

The Tacoma PD? Why would someone running from the law call the cops? She wouldn't.

She also wouldn't lie about calling the cops to get his sympathy. A fabrication like that could be too easily traced.

Could she have been telling the truth after all?

Damn.

He sprinted after her, right back into the storm.

Chapter 5

"I told William we shouldn't travel in this storm." An older woman gripped the tour bus driver's hand as she disembarked.

Dee held the lodge door open as the driver braced the frail woman with a hand to her back. Idling in the parking lot, the silver bus chugged exhaust into the night. Snowflakes danced in the headlight beams.

After Jacob's damning disbelief, she'd dashed from his apartment straight into a rolling tide of guests swelling through the door in search of a warm room. She'd absorbed the sight of that tour bus like a piece of salvation rumbling a diesel tune in the parking lot.

Dee tucked her hands in her pockets. She should

have held her temper in check. Perhaps she should have concocted a story to tide him over until he'd driven her into Tacoma. But she couldn't ignore the sense of urgency to discover if she had a child out there who needed her.

Not that she could have convinced him, anyway. He'd looked like a six-foot-four-inch immovable wall, with his jaw set and eyes so cold. He didn't appear any more approachable now, towering behind the registration desk sorting through the crowd of exhausted travelers. Casting the periodic brooding stare her way. Like now.

Dee studied the bus driver, deciding on the best approach for bumming a ride. The guy was somewhere in his early fifties perhaps, with sandy-gray hair. His patience with the older lady boded well.

Time to start begging. "Do you need some help?"

The driver glanced up. "Oh, hi. Just keep catching the door there, would ya?"

"Sure." Dee pressed her back against the frosted glass.

The driver's eyes flickered over Dee with appreciation as he guided the woman inside. "Thanks. Only another thirty-five more people to go."

Dee gave him the obligatory laugh. He offered a light chuckle in return.

Jacob glanced over from the registration desk and frowned.

Tough. She refused to be moved by his proprietary scowl. He'd had his shot at playing Sir Galahad, and he'd blown it.

Although could she really blame him? Would she have believed someone who told her the same story? She honestly didn't know.

Dee tucked her coat tighter around herself and turned to the driver. "Can you spare a minute to talk?" A smile picked up the corners of his mouth. She needed to squelch those ideas fast. "I could use a ride into town."

His eyes crinkled with the rest of his smile. "Stranded, huh? Wouldn't be the first time I've run into that with this remote route. Let me get these folks unloaded first, then we'll see what we can work out."

"Thank you." There went the rest of her money. But she no longer had time to wait for a more cost-effective alternative. She had to get into Tacoma, fast, and Jacob had decided to turn stubborn.

Okay, she'd turned irritable. But his suspicions had hurt, a lot.

Her mind wandered to the moment he'd held her hand, his touch surprisingly gentle for such a large man. Her body had stirred with an odd mix of hope, security and a dangerous yearning she didn't dare explore.

Then he'd asked for her real name.

Hitching a ride on the tour bus offered her best choice. She didn't have the energy or brain power to spare on complications, and Jacob Stone grew more complicated with each falling snowflake.

Dee stifled the well of exhaustion and moved to assist the remaining thirty-five disembarking seniors.

* * *

An hour later, Dee trudged through the parking lot to her room. After the last of the guests had checked in, she'd pigeonholed the bus driver to cement their plans.

Jacob had darted pensive scowls their way, frowns she'd ignored. If only her jittery stomach could have been as easily controlled.

Talking with the driver, she hadn't dared discuss her amnesia this time, merely saying her boyfriend had ditched her in the motel and she needed a ride into town to file a police report against the abusive jerk. She hated lying, but the cover story sounded good for getting her where she needed to go.

The driver had agreed to her offer of twenty dollars since he would be driving a few blocks out of his way. By midafternoon tomorrow, she would be at the station.

Tugging her key free from her coat pocket, she counted along the doors until she came to her room number.

And the dark shadow lounging outside.

A six-foot-four-inch shadow.

"Convince me." Jacob's gravelly bass mingled with the wind whistling through the eaves.

"What?"

"Convince me you're telling the truth."

Like she could convince this rock of anything. Dee stuffed her key in the lock. "I'd rather go ice swimming."

"Very mature."

She twisted her doorknob. "Good night."

"Quit running away." He angled toward her, his

shoulders blocking the meager parking lot lights as well as the force of the wind. "I'm trying to help you. You have to admit the amnesia thing's pretty far-fetched."

Did he have to be so persuasive and big and sexy? The heat of him seeped into her while the wind whipped around his body.

She flattened her back against the door. "I can't change the truth to suit your idea of believable scenarios."

"What about—" Shivering, he hunched his shoulders deeper into his jacket. "Do we have to talk out here? Wind chill's gotta be ten below."

Being alone with him in a room with beds didn't seem wise. Neither did freezing to death. If he'd planned to hurt her, he could have done so any number of times throughout their day alone together.

Bottom line, she wanted him to believe her.

Dee twisted the knob, backing the door open. "Come on in."

Following her, Jacob ducked inside. Her room wasn't small, but Jacob filled it all the same.

She draped her coat on the edge of the first bed, turned up the heat, considered what to say and why it was so important that he believe her this time. Jacob lounged against the wall until she sat at the small table, then lowered himself into the chair across from her, silently.

Words churned inside her, but she stifled them. Better to let him set the tone.

Jacob stretched his legs in front of him. "What did the Tacoma police have to say when you called them?"

"How did you know I— Oh, the three dollars." She'd forgotten about that part of her tirade. Apparently her mouth ran away from her in the midst of a good rant, another element of her personality to file away with the good and bad she'd deciphered so far.

"Well?"

"They said I need to come in. I described myself, and they did concede there weren't any obvious missing persons' reports to match me. They'll run my prints and do a more thorough search when I get there."

"You're willing to let them fingerprint you and run your picture."

"Absolutely." Dee leaned forward, sensing she might finally be making headway. "Jacob, I don't have a tidy explanation for you. I woke up in this room, alone and scared out of my mind. I had to look at the telephone book to find out where I was. There wasn't even a purse or wallet with identification. Just a little money and this." She scooped her hand into the neck of her sweater, pulling free the necklace. "The closest I could even come to a name is a tarnished *D*. For the last time, I swear to you I don't know who I am."

A piercing stare later, he asked, "Why didn't you say something this morning? Why scrub bathroom floors all day?"

"Have you looked at yourself in the mirror lately? You're pretty darned intimidating, and I'm pretty darned vulnerable."

The first hint of a smile eased through his perpetual scowl. "Okay, I can buy that. But what changed your mind? I didn't magically shrink."

She resisted the urge to rub her stomach. The police would have to know about the possibility of a child since it might help, but she wasn't ready to share something so private. She settled for part of the truth. "Watching you with Emily and Madison made you seem more approachable."

He crossed his feet at the ankles and studied his boots until Dee thought she might spring across the table and shake him.

Jacob glanced to Dee, the furrows smoothing from his brow. "So you have amnesia."

A sigh racked through her. He believed her. He didn't look happy about it, but she could live with that. No matter what she'd done before, he didn't think she was a liar. "Yes. I do," she whispered, her mind screaming, *And I'm so scared. Help me, please.*

Jacob watched the fear flood her face. Any second, he expected her eyes to fill with tears.

They never did. Every line of her body cried out her grief all the same.

He set his caged instincts free. His gut told him to trust her and not let old defensiveness rule him. Simply accept her story. If his instincts were wrong, he would only be out a ride into town.

If his instincts were right, this woman needed him,

badly. A woman who balked at asking for a pair a shoes, needed him.

Something primal stirred within him, latched on and wouldn't let go. Caveman in action? Maybe. Who was he to fight nature? Especially when it came in such an appealing package. "Let's go back to our original plan then. I'll run you into town tomorrow."

"Thank you." She twisted the necklace around her fingers until they turned bloodless. "What about the motel? Who'll take care of the desk?"

"My regular cleaning lady should be back tomorrow. She can handle checkouts and then carry the cordless for incoming calls while she cleans. We'll leave early so we have plenty of daylight if the weather turns rogue again. You need to be looked over by a doctor before we head to the station—"

"Hold on! I just want a ride, not a cavalry charge."

"What do you know about your medical history?"

She winced.

"What if you're a diabetic?" he pressed. "Or have some other condition? Head injuries can cause all sorts of problems. You need to have a doctor check you over. I have an old squadron pal stationed here. He's married to a flight surgeon."

She sagged in her seat. "Good point. But do you have to be so pushy?"

A grin tugged through, easing the knot in his stomach. "Military bluntness."

He wouldn't have to help her long. She must have

family or a boss wondering over her unexplained absence. Or a husband.

Jacob shied away from that thought like the plague.

His gaze snapped to her hand. She wasn't sporting a wedding band or a cheater mark on the pale, slim finger. Small consolation since he knew that wasn't proof positive. Meanwhile, he needed to keep her safe until the police could match her with a missing persons' report.

He could control his attraction. He had to. She needed him, whether she wanted to admit it or not.

Which meant keeping constant watch over her.

If she had some illness lurking, he couldn't let her sleep in her hotel room by herself. Even a simple head trauma necessitated being monitored through the night—by him. Jacob wasn't sure what would be more difficult, convincing Dee that he should stay with her, or resisting the urges that coursed through him while he shared her room for the night.

One fact shone through without question. She wasn't sleeping alone.

"Sleeping with me at the apartment will be more convenient than your room." Jacob crossed his feet at the ankles.

"What?" Dee's hands clenched in the loose folds of her oversize sweatpants.

She did bristle easily. He linked his fingers over his stomach. "Or we can stay in your room if you prefer, but I'd rather be closer to the registration desk and Emily."

"You can't sleep here."

"Thank God you realized that. These beds aren't long enough for me." He stood and waited. The dazed look hadn't melted from her face yet. "Are you ready? How long does it take to gather up your spare sweats?"

"No time at all, because I'm not gathering anything." Dee held up her hand. "Don't get me wrong, I'm grateful for all you've done. But even if I weren't ready to fall flat on my face, I wouldn't pay you back by sleeping with you."

Sleep with Dee. Now there was an enticing image. This probably wasn't a good time to think about the fact that he'd been six months without sex since breaking off his last relationship. "As appealing as that sounds, it's not what I'm suggesting."

"It's not?"

Did she sound disappointed or was it only his over-active libido leading him into wishful territory? "Given your droopy eyes, you would probably crash before the first kiss, anyway, and wound my ego forever."

A grin tugged at her full pink lips, which in turn tugged at his self-control. Damn it all, she wasn't even his type. He usually went for the more chatty, flamboy-ant sorts who filled the conversation, which left him free to stay quiet.

This woman had *listener* written all over her.

Tucking her into bed, alone, was the smarter move.

"I'm talking wake-ups every two hours in case you have a concussion. It's easier if we stay in the same place, rather than me tromping through the parking lot in fifty below wind chill to wake you up to count my fingers."

Strawberry-red crawled up her face. "You must think I'm a paranoid granny."

"I think you're alone and don't know who to trust." Hell no, she wasn't paranoid. He wanted nothing more than to rip the bedspread off one of those mattresses and tangle his body with hers. But a rivaling need churned inside him, a need to protect her, find out who had handled this woman so carelessly.

He tipped her chin with his knuckle. "I promise, I'm not going to jump you while you're passed out."

Did she know that she kept moving ever so slightly against his touch while she stared into his eyes? Just when he considered extending his reach and cupping her face in his palm, she nodded, leaning back. "Thank you. Again."

"Okay, then." Restless, Jacob stood and paced around the room, snagged her coat, turned the heat down. He yanked the door open. "Let's get moving."

Frigid air blasted them. The wind nearly lifted Dee off her feet like Mary Poppins. Jacob allowed himself to drape an arm around her shoulders as they charged across the parking lot, sleet and snow stinging his skin.

Lord, she felt good against him.

Inside the lobby, Dee dipped from under his arm

without meeting his gaze. "I'll just get some extra sheets," she mumbled as she all but sprinted for the supply closet.

Jacob shut off the coffeemaker and followed slowly. He found Dee tucking the beddings along the sofa cushions. He braced a shoulder against the archway leading from the hall to the living area. "Thanks. But I can take care of that myself. I'm going to catch up on some paperwork out front, then I'll probably end up falling asleep in the recliner."

She didn't stop.

"What do you think you're doing?"

Dee sank to the edge of the couch and slid off her shoes. "Going to bed?"

"Right. Bed." He jabbed a thumb over his shoulder toward the loft. "In case you hadn't noticed, it's over there."

Her jaw set. "*Your* bed is over there. *My* bed is here."

"I don't think so."

Her tennis shoes thumped to the floor. "I knew you would be this way. Don't you get tired of being so predictable? Stop with the male strutting ritual. A recliner isn't a bed. If your feet hang off the edge of the motel room beds, you really can't expect to fold yourself onto this sofa. I'm almost half your size. The couch is fine for me."

The woman would argue with a rock.

"Dee, I'm going to be up most of the night anyway. You might as well be comfortable."

"I won't be able to sleep if you're on the sofa or in a chair."

Jacob almost laughed. Her eyelids were millimeters away from sliding closed. She'd be asleep sitting up if he kept talking.

He shifted his weight to one leg. Why not let her think she'd won? He could move her after she zonked out, probably less than sixty seconds from now. "Okay. Have it your way. Enjoy the couch."

"Thanks. I will." She lined her shoes with precision beside the sofa. After a self-conscious glance over her shoulder, she whipped the sweater over her head, unveiling the T-shirt beneath.

Carefully she folded the sweater into an exact square and put it on top of her pile of meager possessions. Seeing her take such care with cast-off clothing, Jacob wanted to buy out Macy's.

Dee slid beneath the sheets, tugging the blankets up to her chin. He watched her eyelids flicker. Just sixty seconds and temptation would be deeply asleep.

Jacob shoved away from the archway and flipped off the light switch, leaving only the fluorescent bulb over the stove on. Moonbeams filtered in through the skylight over his bed.

Sixty seconds suddenly seemed like a hell of a long time.

Burrowing deeper under the blankets, Dee flattened her spine against the sofa back. "Hopefully by tomorrow I'll be sleeping in my own bed. Or maybe I'll be curled up in some bay window, watching the snow and drinking hot cocoa. I think I like hot chocolate with whipped cream. It sounds good, anyway." She sighed, a heavy sound full of resignation. "Someone's got to notice I'm missing soon. A person can't simply disappear without somebody noticing."

"Sure," he lied. He'd seen enough cruelty in the world to know otherwise.

"My family must be so worried." Her words slurred together.

"Of course." Lord, he hoped so.

"We'll call the station again in the morning before we set out for the hospital." Her breathing grew slower, deeper with each word.

"First thing. Bet you'll be glad to see the last of that cleaning bucket."

She seemed to have drifted off, so he eased forward a step. Dee burrowed her head into the pillow, and he hesitated.

"What did he look like?" she whispered.

"Pardon?"

"The man who left me here. What did he look like?"

Jacob called to mind the face of the man who'd signed the register, a scumbag he very much wanted to deck. "About five foot ten. Medium build. Midthirties with blond hair." He struggled to remember more about a guy he'd seen for all of about five minutes. "His clothes looked expensive, good quality Gore-Tex as if he knew what he needed for this kind of weather. And no wedding ring."

Now that he thought about it, he remembered glancing at the guy's finger since he'd checked in as a Mr. and Mrs. "I wish I could give you more."

Especially since it was her only hope for a link to her old life. Even if the link sucked, big-time.

"I guess it's too much to hope for that he got lost looking for morning coffee." Her voice faded into a final shaky sigh.

A tiny, scared sigh that stabbed clean through him.

"We'll find out who you are," he vowed.

No answer.

Jacob stepped away from the kitchen counter.

Sixty seconds complete. Dee's chest rose and fell in the even pattern of heavy sleep. He ambled over and knelt beside her.

Only in his life for one day and he would never forget her. What made her so special? Sure she was pretty, but not a knockout by technical standards. And she was so delicate—but stubborn.

She had a fire and grit he respected. No whining or clinging-vine crap; she'd pulled herself through a day that would have sent most people diving into a bottle of Valium.

Jacob eased his arms under her, slowly, watching for signs of stirring. There weren't any. She'd fallen asleep hard and fast, her slender body deadweight.

Dead? His gut fisted. He'd been so concerned with concussions, he hadn't considered foul play.

He should have considered that straight up. Jacob

forced himself to recall every detail of "Mr. Smith's" face, his vehicle. Hopefully the Suburban plate number could be traced. He had it on file.

And if it couldn't be traced… That implied a danger for Dee he didn't even want to consider.

Jacob tucked her more securely against his chest. He couldn't stop himself from dropping his head closer and inhaling, tightening his grip and savoring her softness she'd hidden beneath the sweater all day.

If John Smith had wanted her dead, it wouldn't have been difficult. There must be another answer, and they would find it at the police station.

He would help her through the police procedural red tape in a way her tour bus buddy never could. The Tacoma PD would damn well do their best to find out who this Dee Smith/Jane Doe was. He would make sure of that.

Gently he lowered her to his bed. He draped the quilt over her and stroked the hair from her face. Silky strands slid through his fingers, glistening in the beams shimmering through the skylight. His battered knuckles skimmed petal-soft skin.

A man could lose himself in her softness.

But she needed to remember her past, and he was a man who wanted to leave his behind.

Standing by the lobby coffee machine, Dee sunk her teeth into a cream-filled chocolate doughnut. She would vacuum carpets until the end of time for more of these.

She stared at Jacob through the plate-glass window as he warmed his truck for their trip into town. All faded denim and elemental power, he made her mouth water for more than doughnuts.

Jacob's deep voice had reached to her through the night, comforting, protecting, wrapping itself around her like the quilt. She might not have always known where she was, but his voice had anchored her as she embraced another snippet of sleep.

Man, she was hungry, ravenous, wide-awake and better rested than she could ever remember feeling. A laugh snuck free. Like that was a stretch given she had a little over twenty-four hours' worth of memories.

What had he thought as he'd moved her to his bed? The notion of him carrying her was both frustrating and more than a bit exciting.

Putting that first horrible day behind her made the world seem full of possibilities. It was okay to lean on Jacob, just a little. They were only riding into town together.

She watched him prepare the truck. Methodical. Steady. He moved with even-paced determination. He stepped from the cab, leaving the blue Ford running, puffy clouds billowing from the exhaust pipe.

Snow dusted his jet-black hair and shoulders. He really should wear a hat. She almost grabbed one for him, but stopped herself. She could already envision his sleepy-lidded look if she shouted out the door to him like some overprotective mother or schoolteacher.

His arms reached an impossibly long stretch across the windshield to scrape ice. Just below the waist of his navy ski parka, his jeans pulled taut against his backside. Chocolate melted in her mouth, warm and full over her taste buds.

Jacob knelt to disconnect the electrical cord from the block heater and thoughts of long, chocolate-flavored kisses slid away.

Block heater. A unique piece of equipment. The special addition to cold-weather-area vehicles to protect the battery. That wasn't standard information except for someone who lived in extreme climates.

Yes. She wanted to dance. A real clue. Maybe more would come to her throughout the day. And if she were from this region, that would make locating her all the easier.

Background information. A small bit, but so important to a woman with little enough to call her own, and a driving need to find out if she had a child.

Dee dashed for the door, ready to share her revelation. "Jacob, guess what?"

He turned to her, snowflakes hanging on those long lashes of his. For a moment, no clouds darkened his eyes, just a pale, clear blue for her to fly into.

She forgot how to talk. Thinking became temporarily optional, as well, while she let his eyes glide over her.

Dee cleared her throat. She pointed to the cord dangling from the truck grill. "That's a block heater."

He blinked. His blue eyes became moody and impenetrable again. "Uh, yeah."

"A *block heater.* I know what it is. I can see one in my head. I have one. I must be from the North, or was at some time."

A half smile kicked up one corner of his mouth. "Good, good. Go with it. What does the car look like?"

Dee closed her eyes and thought, hard. Squinting though one eye at Jacob, she said, "Brown, maybe?"

"Okay. Model? Make?"

She grappled for the memory. She should have chased the thought while it was fresh.

"Sorry." She shook her head. "It's gone now."

"That's all right." His hand cupped her shoulder. "You did well. Don't force it. It's a positive sign you're remembering bits and pieces."

"I hope so." The weight of his hands reassured her enough to push out the question she'd been afraid to ask but had to have answered. "Did you see Mr. Smith's car when he checked in?"

Jacob's broad hand cupped her shoulder. "White Suburban. I checked my files this morning, and he had dealer plates, in-state."

"Not great, but maybe the police can still track him."

She looked up into those wolflike eyes, eyes that had greeted her hourly during the night.

With a final squeeze, Jacob's hand fell away. "Emily's got the front desk until Grace arrives in another half hour. Let's hit the road."

Her shoulder felt bare without his comforting touch. She hadn't known to miss that comfort three seconds ago. How silly to mourn its loss now.

"Are you ready, Dee?"

"What?" Dee roused herself from a blatant stare at his bare head with its beautiful hair and reddened ears. "Yeah, just let me grab one more thing from inside."

Dee gripped the rail for balance as she dashed up the steps. Without giving herself time to think why, she headed straight for the coatrack and snatched Jacob's hat.

Chapter 6

"**W**ho's your doctor friend?" After over a half hour of ten-ton silence, Dee tried yet another attempt to jump-start a conversation. This guy had pensive down to an art form, and she needed a distraction from the nerves eating up her stomach lining.

"What?" Jacob glanced from the road to Dee sitting in the truck cab beside him. The knit cap lay between them on the tan tweed seat.

"Tell me more about the doctor I'll be seeing." She shifted to face Jacob.

Jacob hooked his wrist over the steering wheel. For a moment, it seemed he wouldn't answer, merely let the telephone poles whiz by at a monotonous pace. A toolbox in the backseat rattled in the silence. "Like I said before, she's the wife of an old crewmate from South Carolina. He's stationed here at McChord Air Force Base in Tacoma now. Actually they both are since she's a military doctor—Kathleen Bennett."

From the solemn set of his jaw, he probably wanted to drop her and all her problems. Although it stung being considered little more than a nuisance, she couldn't blame him for not wanting to chat it up with his annoying amnesiac tenant. "I've imposed on you enough. Let's go straight to the police station."

His gaze slid from the road to her with the slow shake of his head. "Your health comes first."

"I'm tired of waiting for answers. I need a name, a real name." She couldn't stop the notion that she wanted to meet Jacob on a more even footing, as an independent woman meeting an intriguing, sexy man, rather than the whole dependency scenario. "Besides, I won't have insurance until we know who I am."

"Doc Bennett won't charge you anything. I already called ahead."

Frustration made her want to clench her fists and pitch an unholy tantrum. "While I appreciate your help, I should have some say in my own life."

"Sorry." His mouth curved into one of those rare, one-sided smiles. "Of course you should."

What would a full wicked smile that twinkled in his eyes look like? This wasn't the kind of distraction she needed. "Let's go to the station now, please."

"Think for a minute. You've been in contact with the Tacoma PD every couple of hours and nothing's coming through. They're running the license plate from the Suburban now. I didn't want to scare you when we discussed it before, but we need to be sure nothing's seriously wrong. Finding out who you are won't be worth a damn if you pass out on the precinct floor."

Perhaps his one-word answers hadn't been so bad after all. "But wouldn't I have already—"

"That's for the doctor to say."

"Fine." She waved a hand. "You're right, and I'm irritable. There's so much beyond my control, I can't stop grasping at any little thing I can manage. Does that make any sense?"

His smile faded altogether. "Yeah."

Back to one-word answers. So much for conversation.

Dee stared out over the endless stretch of snow road, mountain peaks just visible through the misty fog. She monitored the mile markers, city limits now only ten miles away.

Anticipation tingled through her at the notion of discovering her identity and hopefully answers about a possible child. Even so, she couldn't stop a sliver of regret from mingling into the mix. Regaining her memory could mean saying goodbye to Jacob.

Jacob was more than ready to say goodbye to whoever had been following them since they'd left the Lodge.

The snowy haze made it difficult to keep track of cars

around them beyond headlights beaming through soupy weather. But he'd seen the same light-colored SUV peek through the fog again and again. He couldn't be sure of the paint job with all the sludge on the vehicle, but he also couldn't stop thinking about Mr. Smith's white Suburban.

Of course with so many SUVs around here, the odds of seeing slush-covered Suburbans were high. It could be coincidence. He'd tried slowing, speeding up, even taking a side road and still he could swear they had a tail.

He didn't want to stress out Dee further, especially not before a doctor's okay on her health. At least she wasn't pressing for conversation anymore and he could keep his full attention on making sure they made it to the base safe and sound.

No one would get through the front gate without proper identification.

He checked the rearview mirror again. Nothing but snow and a sedan now. Still, the unease itched. Maybe he was being overly cautious.

But until he knew what had happened to Dee, he couldn't relax his guard.

"There are no drugs in your system."

Dr. Kathleen Bennett's words brought Dee a mixed swell of relief and disappointment. Relief over nothing toxic in her system, and disappointment that the answer wouldn't be simple.

She took in the military doctor, a flight surgeon who

wore a green flight suit with a stethoscope around her neck. The woman inspired trust with a brisk no-nonsense confidence that Dee appreciated. She would focus on that, trust that and try not to think overlong about Dr. Bennett's slight swell of pregnancy that made Dee's stomach clench.

She forced back the need to take Jacob's hand. While he'd sat in the waiting room throughout her morning full of exams, she'd asked that he be allowed to join her afterward.

Watching him walk so confidently through his military world at McChord Air Force Base sparked confidence in her—and a yen to see him in *his* flight suit.

"I'll send your blood work out for more extensive testing, but so far there's nothing out of the ordinary." Dr. Bennett tucked her pen behind her ear into her red braid and flipped through the chart. "You've definitely got a bump on you head, but not severe enough for us to be concerned about."

Jacob swallowed, a long, slow ripple of muscle along his strong neck.

He was worried? For her? He'd hidden it well earlier in the truck, so distant and moody, only relaxing somewhat once they crossed through the front gate of the base.

Regardless, she wanted to clutch his hand in gratitude rather than for comfort. Someone cared what happened to her. How small and incredible a thought.

Jacob pressed, "When will we hear back?"

"A week at the most."

Dee winced. "So many tests. Expensive tests."

"Don't worry. We've got it covered."

Jacob had, she must mean, but Dee couldn't afford to argue. "Thank you."

Dr. Bennett flipped another page on the chart. "Your psychiatric evaluation came back basically normal."

An airplane roared overhead and Dee flinched. Just the jolt of the unexpected noise, right? Not freaking out with a panic attack, damn it. Still she had to ask, "Basically?"

"You're displaying moderate signs of anxiety, but that's perfectly normal given the situation. I'd be more concerned if you weren't at all stressed by the circumstances."

A calm settled over her for the first time. "You believe me."

Her brows rose. "Oh, yes, you passed that part of the psyche eval with flying colors. I can prescribe something for the anxiety."

"No. Thank you." A thought occurred to her. "Although I was carrying an EpiPen with me and I have no idea what I'm allergic to."

Dr. Bennett frowned. "Were you wearing a medical alert bracelet?"

A good thought on the doctor's part, but, "No, and I haven't found one anywhere in my room."

She pulled her pen from behind her ear. "It could be any one of a million things. The most common allergies I see are to bees, peanuts and shellfish. You should probably avoid those and keep the epinephrine close. I'll send you home with a few extra to keep around, just in case one gets lost. I'll also give you a printout of symptoms to be aware of in case of an allergic reaction."

Dee slid her hand into her pocket, her fist closing around the medicine. "Thank you."

"All right, then." The doctor scribbled a notation on her chart, then tucked the pen back into her red braid. "You've managed well so far, but don't hesitate to let me know if something changes."

Jacob stepped from behind the gurney as if to block the door. "That's all you have for us?"

The doctor's hand fell to rest on the barely visible pregnancy bulge as if to soothe a restless child. "To be honest, Dee, I can't explain why you're suffering a memory loss. Until you remember, we have no way of knowing. On the bright side, you're a healthy young woman, somewhere in your early thirties, I would guess. You've had your appendix and tonsils removed. You're O Positive and don't wear glasses. You weren't battered, attacked or raped. No signs of a sexually transmitted disease."

She paused, shuffling uncomfortably for the first time.

Dee couldn't take her eyes off that hand circling a pregnant stomach. She already knew the answer before she asked the question. "And?"

"You've been pregnant at least once, delivering by Cesarean section."

Dee exhaled, surprised how hearing what she already knew still sucker punched her. A baby. A child. Son or daughter. She squeezed her eyes shut for three calming breaths.

She opened her eyes and found Jacob's hands clenched by his sides. She should have prepared him for this. It hadn't been fair to surprise him, but how could she have slid it into polite conversation? *By the way, I have this nifty scar on my belly that leads me to believe I've had a baby or two. Oh, yeah, and don't forget the sexy stretch marks.*

Jacob cleared his throat. "Any idea when?"

"Not recently, judging by the incision. Again, I'm sorry I can't do more for you than that."

Jacob pivoted on his boot heels toward Dee, and she turned away. She couldn't face any more questions from Jacob, not yet. "Thank you, Doctor. At least I know I'm not dying or crazy. That's something, right?"

"Yes, it is." The doctor squeezed Dee's arm.

But it wasn't enough. She wasn't content to let time take its course and hope someone might be looking for her. She had a child to find.

She'd also started a new life, a life rapidly filling with people, responsibilities and debts to repay. Emotional as well as financial. To do that, she needed to hop off the gurney and stop feeling sorry for herself. She pulled her attention back to the doctor's words.

"Jacob, I want to take a look at your arm before you two head out to the police station. And don't bother to tell me you're fine. I know all about the ego you boys tote around, and I'm not backing down."

Jacob's arm. How could she have forgotten his injury just because he'd ditched his sling? She'd been so immersed in her own mess that she hadn't even given him any warning of what they would hear. She was being selfish, especially after all he'd done for her.

Now if she could just scavenge some communication skills she had no way of knowing she possessed.

Hunger roared to life within him, a hunger fired by more than the woman walking beside him as they left the police station and settled into his truck.

They'd filed an official report. During their afternoon at the station, they hadn't learned anything new from the police about her. The cops had actually been more interested in the fact that the Suburban plates hadn't appeared in any data bank. Had Mr. Smith written down the wrong number by accident or on purpose? No way of knowing.

Jacob gripped the steering wheel tighter. He'd done all he could for today. With a trip to the doctor and the cops. Now he couldn't avoid thinking about what they'd learned from Doc Bennett.

Dee had a child.

Just when he'd thought he couldn't be surprised anymore, there came the latest bombshell. Jacob slid the key into the ignition and cranked the engine. He hooked his arm along the seat, turning to look out the rear window as he backed out.

Seeing Dee stopped him cold.

She wasn't crying, not outwardly. She simply sat, her fingers gripping the lap belt over her stomach. And she was shaking, not much, but enough for him to notice. Her teeth began chattering.

"The heat should kick in soon."

She nodded tightly, her face front, her gaze veering neither left nor right.

He slid the truck back into Park. "You okay?"

Dee nodded again.

"You're scaring me a little here."

Her head tucked, the bare curve of her neck showing through the glide of her hair. "It's a lot to take in. That's all. I'll be fine. How's your arm?"

"I'm cleared to go back to work when my leave's over in a couple of weeks."

"That's wonderful. I'm so relieved to hear it."

Dee's fists squeezed around the seat belt until her knuckles shone white as the tender line of her neck. He'd watched plenty of women pump out tears over the years, but he'd never seen one try so valiantly *not* to cry.

It caught him like a quick uppercut to the jaw. Anger began to take a backseat to sympathy and something else. Something dangerous that lured him to sling an arm along the back of her seat. "You're not fine."

She dipped her head lower and mumbled, "Rocket scientist as well as military hero and motel mogul."

Jacob felt a chuckle escape. How could he not admire her grit? He should have realized she'd fire back, a way of going numb rather than launching into overemotionalism.

He notched a knuckle under her chin and lifted her

face. "We're going to find out who you are. And we're going to find out about your child. I know you don't always welcome my help, hell, anyone's help, but I'm in for the long haul. Understand?"

She shrugged away, swiping the back of her hand across her eyes. "I'm sorry for not telling you before about the C-section scar."

At least she'd begun to thaw, not that it relieved him the way it should have. "I know now, and we're doing all we can. The world won't end if we sit tight for a few minutes while you have a good cry."

"Sobbing my eyes out won't fix anything."

She had that much right. Why then did he want to convince her she needed a good three-hanky vent?

Jacob unbuckled her seat belt and allowed himself to cup her shoulders. Even through her coat, he could feel her fragile bones, but he now knew she had a steely spine for support.

He tugged her toward him. "Come here."

She resisted, as he'd known she would.

"I just need to hold you for a second, okay?"

Her back bowed as she angled away. "Why?"

He reminded himself he was only convincing her because she needed to be held. Not because he was locked in the grip of some fierce longing to press her against him and reassure himself. "Because you're all right. I was worried about you. And because I know you must be scared as hell wondering if you have a kid out there somewhere!"

Dee sniffled and Jacob smiled, not because he was glad she'd begun crying but because for once he understood her. He could handle tears, dish out comfort. He pulled her to his chest. His forehead fell to rest against her hair. Motel shampoo mixed with the lingering antiseptic scent of the hospital.

For years, he'd accepted that the honed instinct to protect couldn't be shut off at the end of a mission. The need to protect the woman in his arms throbbed through him. It scoured him, tearing away boundaries, leaving behind something more basic, fundamental, elemental.

His hand traveled up to cradle the back of her head, his fingers massaging her scalp. The very feel of her sizzled up his arm, shooting straight through him with a need he'd stamped down for longer than he cared to remember.

God, he wanted her. Not that he could do a thing about it. The woman had just been subjected to a traumatic morning filled with an invasive physical and a police interrogation.

With shaky restraint, Jacob fenced in his own needs and continued rubbing gentle, small circles into her head. A moan whispered from her lips, nothing much, just a small little breath of sound.

A small sound that charged the air.

Her fingers dug into his arms, tighter, then crawled to his shoulders and into his hair. She tilted her face just as she pulled his down to meet her.

What the hell? He'd promised himself he wouldn't do this.

But *he* wasn't. *She* was.

"Thank you, Jacob." She skimmed her lips over his.

Cradling her to him, still half-afraid she might be as fragile as she looked, Jacob brushed her mouth with his in a tender salute. The thread of longing between them pulled tauter, drawing him deeper. Gently he traced her lips, then teased her tongue with his, tasting morning coffee and acquainting himself with the unique flavor of Dee.

She flattened herself to him. Her fingers gripped the neck of his shirt and tugged, hard. "More."

So much for thoughts of restraint.

His mouth settled over hers with a firm rightness he could have never predicted, and wasn't quite sure he could handle while maintaining any semblance of sanity.

Dee all but wrapped herself around him as she kissed him back, fiercely, with an intensity that rocked all his plans for reserve. Maybe he'd thawed her a little too much. Her kisses had a frenzied edge that went beyond passion.

A chill settled over Jacob. She didn't really want him, just somebody, anybody to shake her from the numbing sensation that had come from her messed-up life.

Talk about the proverbial bucket of cold water. If— when—he made love to her it wouldn't be in the front seat of a truck, and it wouldn't be because she was running from something.

He wanted her running *to* him.

"Dee, we have to stop." With more than a little regret, he untwined her arms from around his neck. "We're in a parking lot."

And damned if that didn't make him start looking over his shoulder again as he'd done during their drive into town. Luckily nobody appeared to be paying any attention to a truck with fogged windows.

She stiffened, then flung herself away against the seat. "I can't believe I did that. Like you haven't already got a thousand reasons to think all sorts of crazy things about me, I go adding more ammo to the impression."

"I'm not thinking anything other than you needed to blow off some steam, and this isn't the right way. It's okay." Well, it wasn't, but it would be once he could suck in a few more breaths.

Her sigh rippled through the air before she nodded and smiled, a wry, wobbly grin that caressed his hand. "What a first kiss, huh?"

"What?"

"My first kiss. Even if I've been kissed a thousand times before, it's not like I remember any of them. So this is it. My new first. Is that strange or what?"

"Or what." A new chill seeped through Jacob, dousing his need more effectively than a dive into a snowbank.

Yes, he wanted her, and he couldn't help but notice she might want him a little in return. But they had a problem.

He'd considered any number of reasons why he shouldn't lunge across the truck cab and convince her to find the nearest bed—or even ask her out to dinner and a movie. She had a life out there somewhere. He had a mess of a life here.

But he hadn't considered one fundamental reason to tread warily, if at all.

This woman beside him, a woman who signed into a motel as "Mrs. Smith," a woman who'd given birth to a child, a woman who might well have a husband, this woman was for all intents and purposes—a virgin.

Chapter 7

He hated that damned virtuous act of hers. Of anyone, he knew how she really acted in bed.

His foot pressed the accelerator, the SUV's tires gripping for traction even with the four-wheel drive. He forced his focus back on the road as he neared the Lodge. He just needed to see her, find out what she was doing, be sure she wasn't making it with some other guy.

Everybody should know what a slut she was. They should hear the truth about her, but he couldn't tell them. He'd needed to be attentive, loving. Appearances mattered. What people thought of him mattered if he ever wanted to put his life back together again.

He turned off the highway onto the side road, hunting rifles rattling in the floorboards as he bumped and jostled toward the out-of-the-way restaurant. All he'd wanted was money and a way out of the ball-and-chain life he'd been stuck with.

So why didn't he just leave? Loose ends. If it weren't for their kid, he would have walked away from her a long time ago.

He couldn't wait for luck to turn his way any longer. He needed to take fate into his own hands.

Dee stared out the truck window. She wanted to ask more about Jacob's military world, a place where he felt comfortable, even if the gates and fences and airplanes roaring overhead left her feeling a bit claustrophobic. But Jacob was even more reticent than he'd been on the drive earlier.

Perhaps the icy roads simply demanded his full attention.

At first, she'd wondered if Jacob's moodiness could be a by-product of her having thrown herself at him. What had she been thinking? Obviously she hadn't been thinking of anything but soaking up the comfort of his strength.

Dee spun thoughts of him over and over as they drove along the gravel road toward Marge's Diner. She could imagine him in a uniform. The mental picture was more than a little exciting, the brooding, twenty-first-century warrior. It seemed right somehow.

The same man running a motel for years on end... That image didn't gel at all. Already she recognized his need for action, his inescapable manner of taking charge. It wasn't frenzied, just even-paced, steady, as he took care of everything from filing a police report to making sure she remembered to eat.

Jacob slowed the truck, wheels crunching across the diner's parking lot. Trucks and Suburbans dominated the unmarked spaces. A replica of a prairie schoolhouse sat perched by a lake. The candy-apple-red building splashed color onto the otherwise gray mountainous horizon. A pier spiked out of the frozen waters, providing a narrow wooden path above the sheet of ice.

Not at all what she'd expected.

She'd been looking for some fifties throwback diner with jukeboxes and counter service. Had she subconsciously substituted something from her own hometown into expectations for Jacob's area? She reached into her mental recesses in hope of finding the face of her child....

Jacob parked between a pair of slush-caked 4X4s. "Ready to eat?"

"What?" The shadowy vision melted like the ice cream she would never see eaten. Disappointment avalanched over her, nearly smothering her with frustration. Dee reached for her seat belt and jabbed at the button. "Yeah. Sorry. I'm actually hungry."

Three jabs later, she still couldn't wrestle the buckle open. Jacob covered her hand with his and released the latch. His hand didn't move away with the seat belt. "Is something wrong?"

"It's nothing." Could have been everything. "I'm just tired of how it feels like a memory is right there, but I can't chase it down."

Absently he caressed the inside of her wrist with a callused finger. "Maybe while we're waiting for supper, we could play some word association games, see if we can stir up your past."

"Good idea." She wanted to imprison his hand. Better yet, haul him back into the truck, into an embrace, the only place she'd been where the insidious whispers of loneliness had faded.

Instead she allowed herself a selfish moment to rest in the heat of his eyes as they studied her, as they held her in a grip equally as powerful as his arms ever could be. His musky scent permeated the interior of the truck, and she breathed in the reassurance of pure Jacob.

Gently he released her hand. "Let's get moving."

So much for making new memories. She would be better served hunting for the old.

Climbing the diner steps, Dee leaned against Jacob's arm until they reached the double doors. Nerves pattered a jig in her stomach. She assumed she understood the basics of etiquette, but she didn't want to embarrass Jacob, even unwittingly.

Part of her wanted to hide out in her dark but familiar motel room until she remembered. Another, stronger part of her insisted she step back into the world if she ever hoped to regain her past and find her child. To do that, she needed Jacob's help. The diner could well provide a wealth of information about him, a man who intrigued her, yet unsettled her. A man she had to trust with everything.

She strode into the restaurant with the long-shot hope that someone might recognize her. The inside of Marge's Diner matched the outside decor. Long, rough-hewn picnic tables filled with customers lined the room, everyone from families to a table of military members in uniforms—more flight suits to torment her imagination. Apparently the appeal of this place enticed people to drive a long way in crummy conditions.

Dishes clanked, and voices mingled. A family of five studied the daily specials posted on a chalkboard over the cash register. The board also listed instructions not to tattle, spit, pinch or pull ponytails.

Dee loved it. She unwrapped her scarf from around her head, a sense of utter rightness coaxing her to step farther inside. She needed a haven, some bit of peace to end a day that had stunk. "Oh, Jacob, this place is great. No wonder it's packed."

"I had a feeling you might like it. You'll have to tell Marge when she brings our order." Jacob followed the waitress as she pointed to the empty table for two in the back.

A table that waited just past a field of inquiring faces. Nerves returning like a bad penny, Dee stumbled back a step. She couldn't shake the notion that someone was staring at her. Maybe they all were.

When they found out about her amnesia, would they label her a liar as Jacob had initially? Or would they think her a nutcase? "Maybe we should order takeout and go back to the motel."

"Fried walleye demands to be eaten while hot."

As he guided her toward the table, Jacob offered nods and offhand greetings to people who called out and slapped him on the back.

A hulking tall man in a green flight suit pushed back from his table and stood. "Hey, Mako, everything must have gone okay at the base. I didn't expect you'd be done so fast."

Jacob stopped, placing a steadying hand between Dee's shoulder blades. "Dee, this big guy is married to Doc Bennett. Bronco, this is Dee."

She extended her hand, preparing for a crushing grip. Yet the aviator shook with a firm but not-too-tight clasp. She'd liked his wife and found she already liked the husband, too. "Your wife was very generous with her time today. I appreciate it more than I can say."

"You're with Mako. That makes you one of us and we take care of our own."

How much did he know of her problem? She didn't plan to put it out there and he politely didn't ask.

Jacob turned to the other man at the table who was holding a fistful of French fries. "This is Crusty."

The wiry guy cranked a megawatt grin as he dumped

the fries back on his plate, swiped his hand across his flight suit and shook hers with an energetic pump. "Great to meet you. My wife is gonna be torqued that we all got to see you first. Well, and that we saw Mako, too. Maybe you can talk this fella into accepting one of our dinner invitations before he heads back to Charleston."

Dee didn't know what to say to all of that so she simply smiled in return. Within seconds the men were discussing the flight the two had just completed and Dee let herself relax. Then suddenly she didn't feel so calm after all.

Back to Charleston. Somehow she'd forgotten what Emily said about Jacob being stationed somewhere else.

Panic bubbled in her stomach. How could she have become so dependent on a man she'd known for a day and a half? But her life consisted of just those few hours and he'd filled most of them.

She forced her breathing to even out while they finished their conversation. Then, thank goodness, Jacob powered ahead without pausing to give anyone else a chance to ask the questions stamped in their curious eyes. She shook off the uneasy sensation of being gawked at and charged forward.

He held the chair for her before settling across the table. She forced her hands to steady, reminded herself to relax.

With a fingernail, she flicked the edge of a menu that peeked from inside an old school primer. "Can we not tell people about my, uh, memory issue just yet? I don't want that to be everyone's first impression of me— crazy amnesiac lady."

"Whatever lowers your stress level. I didn't say anything to the guys over there, in case you were wondering. I spoke straightaway with the doc and she'll keep patient confidentiality."

"Thank you." Dee stole another glance at the diner's patrons and wondered if everybody would treat her problems with as much care as Jacob had.

Table by table, diners stopped staring and returned to their meals. Except for one group over by the potbellied stove soda dispenser. Emily was standing there, draped over a teenage boy. They were with a group of seemingly normal, everyday kids.

A fragment of Dee's peace edged away. What kind of life did her own child have? Was she missed along with trips to the park and ice-cream parlor? Dee couldn't decide which bothered her more—her child crying for her or not missing her at all.

Jacob drummed his straw against the table absently. "Let's try a word association game."

Anything sounded better than waiting around for her past to magically unveil itself. Of course, it also made her all the more vulnerable to Jacob. What would she reveal unwittingly? "Okay. Ready whenever you are." *Liar.*

"Home."

An empty hall echoed. "House."

"House."

Stenciled cartoon airplanes along a wall. "Nursery."
"Baby."
Love. "Child."
"Husband."
Nothing. She drew a blank. Her head throbbed with
the effort of trying to force an image. She pressed her
fingers to her aching temples. "It's fading."

Jacob touched her elbow. "We'll try again later."

"Sure." Dee swiped her hand over her forehead,
feeling wobbly and caught between two worlds. She
looked around the room to ground herself in the moment.

Her gaze hooked on Emily feeding French fries to
the teenager she guessed to be Chase. His mother must
be watching the baby, because Madison wasn't anywhere in sight. Chase's clothes hung from his frame.
Broad shoulders filled out his oversize T-shirt and open
button-down. Dee couldn't help but think that if Emily
were her daughter, she'd blow that boy out of the water
for putting his hands so low on Emily's hips, especially
in public.

She could see the tension in Jacob's jaw, felt an
echoing frustration. What was the right answer for those
two? She honestly didn't know. They were stuck in
such an awkward age, hiding all those confused feelings
behind too much hair and droopy pants, teenagers trying
on new personas like hats.

Was she much better off? Trying to find pieces of
herself and patch them into a whole person.

Even if she discovered her old identity, she wondered

how much of the new creation she would carry with her. She couldn't imagine emerging from this ordeal as if it had never happened. Certainly her short time knowing Jacob would be imprinted on her brain long after she left Rockfish and this moody man behind.

"Supper was nice." Clouds puffed into the night air as Dee spoke. "Thanks for the fried walleye."

Outside Dee's motel door, Jacob leaned against his truck fender. "No problem."

He watched Dee clutch the doorknob behind her back. Was she reluctant to say good-night, too?

They'd shared a room once, but concerns for her health had offered a substantial cold shower. Tonight, especially after that kiss, his resolve was weakening.

A fleeting image of waking up next to her tormented him. He couldn't leave fast enough. "See you in the morning."

"Jacob—" Her voice reached to him.

Glancing back over his shoulder, he asked, "Yeah?"

"I appreciate your taking me to the diner and introducing me around. I needed that."

"It wasn't anything special." As a matter of fact, it had felt too comfortable.

"Maybe not to you. But to me, it was blessedly normal, kind of like…catching snowflakes on your tongue. Magical in its simplicity. Thank you for that gift."

Then she smiled. Just smiled, but the happiness spread all the way to her eyes.

Her beauty blindsided him like a surprise whiteout.

How could he have ever thought her merely pretty? She radiated something incredible that far surpassed an average word such as "pretty."

A lock of hair slid free from her scarf and lifted with the circling winds. Drawn to Dee in spite of his better judgment, he shoved away from the truck and stopped in front of her. The wind at his back, he shielded her.

Her fingers fluttered upward and landed lightly on his head, dusting snow away. "You really should remember to wear a hat."

He smiled down at her. "Sure, Mom."

Her arm dropped back to her side again. Hurt dimmed her eyes. "Sorry."

"It's okay." He kept forgetting how prickly she could be. He folded the ends of her scarf over each other and resisted the urge to smooth his hands along her shoulders, cup the softness just below her coat. "You need to sleep. You didn't rest much last night."

"Neither did you."

He wouldn't tonight, either, with her scent still clinging to his sheets. Not that it mattered if he washed them. After a day spent together in the truck cab, his senses were saturated with her fragrance.

Dee traced squiggly patterns in the snow with the toe of her tennis shoe. "I enjoyed meeting your friends today. You must be itching to get back to work."

Work which would take him away from here—and her.

A wry grin tugged one side of his face. "Yeah, I have to admit, I miss it, the flying and the camaraderie."

"Even after getting shot?"

"Even then."

"How did it happen?"

The day spread out through his mind, the surprise of it all coming during a low-key mission. "My C-17 was transporting a political contingent across Europe for goodwill visits to a number of countries over the Christmas holidays. On the last stop in Bavaria, some radical crook with an agenda tried to assassinate the—"

"Senator from South Carolina—Ginger Landis." Dee blinked fast, her eyes widening with surprise. "I remember that."

"You do?"

She nodded quickly. "I remember seeing the report on TV—" she snapped her fingers "—a wide-screen television…" Her cheeks puffed, her excitement dimming. "And that's it. The memory of where I was then… It's gone." She shook her head, her gaze focused on him again. "But ohmigod, you were shot. I do remember from the news report that you got some kind of medal for saving an old lady at the ceremony."

Saving the world while his sister needed him more. "I just happened to be in the seat next to someone who needed help. The rest was instinct, not some great heroic decision."

"Yeah, right, whatever." She cocked her head to the side. "How amazing it must feel to make such a big difference in people's lives. No wonder you're itching to get back." She studied her chewed-down fingernails. "Only a couple more weeks until you leave."

"I'm not out the door yet. I need to settle Emily, or convince her to come with me to Charleston until I get a transfer to Tacoma."

"I just assumed she would be going with you...."

"She doesn't want to leave, not even to live in Tacoma." His sister was too enamored with Chase to go even an hour away.

"Isn't she a senior? Graduation is only about four months away."

"She's a junior, Chase is a senior."

"Will he stay?"

"I honestly don't know. She doesn't want to lose any time with him." His jaw flexed. "I haven't been around enough to get a read off of him."

"That's not your fault. You're an adult, living your life." She grazed her fingers just above his gunshot wound. "Putting yourself in harm's way."

"I had some lucky breaks as a teenager. Thanks to joining the local Civil Air Patrol I made connections, found direction in the training and flying along for rescue missions. I got out of here. I need to pay back that debt."

Her face softened with understanding. "You don't like owing anyone anything, do you?"

"Not much." Debts gave over power to someone else and he needed to be in control. "I had hoped Emily would find the same. She was a member of Civil Air

Patrol, too, along with Chase. Then she got pregnant and dropped out."

"I'm sorry about your sister, your father, too." Her puffy breaths met his, entwined and swirled between them, brushing the air with their combined heat. Memories of Dee's mouth on his pulsed through his mind, then lower.

Control would slip away completely if he didn't haul butt away from her. Now. He'd made it halfway to his truck before her voice stopped him.

"Jacob," she called out. "I haven't forgotten that kiss. Something like that is kind of tough to forget, and believe me, I'm an expert at forgetting."

He paused. Snow gathered on his shoulders, he stood still for so long before looking back.

She stuffed her mittened hands in her pockets. "Don't worry, I'm not going to throw myself at you a second time. I just want to talk. I—" she hesitated, before gasping in a deep breath "—I don't want to be alone. All that's waiting for me inside that room is a cold bed and a clean tub. Jacob, my heart hurts when I think of my own child. My arms feel so empty for a baby I can't even remember."

Dee's jaw quivered. "What if I'm a mass murderer? Or a bank robber on the run." Her voice deflated to a whisper. "Or a married woman."

Her words pierced through him as cleanly as the bullet he'd taken in his arm. A person who lived by definitive lines of right and wrong, he knew he couldn't have her until he'd ruled out the possibility of a husband. Damn it, where was the man, and why wasn't he tearing up the world searching for Dee?

With one finger, he traced a slow, deliberate path over her jaw. This woman could make a man forget how to breathe.

His fingers splayed across her cheek.

More than a little regret pulsing through him, he let his hands fall to rest on her shoulders and turned her toward her door. "Go to sleep, Dee."

It was for the best. Her life was complicated enough. She needed his help. She definitely didn't need to plunge into some relationship with a guy who would only be around for two weeks.

She might have been better off cutting her losses and staying in Tacoma after all.

Chapter 8

Dee shoved the lost-and-found box to the back of the closet. Over the past week, the container had filled. Rapidly. Jacob had the most absentminded patrons on the planet. And they all wore a size seven.

She'd been pleased to discover the first pair of jeans and a flannel shirt, yellow with flowers that made her smile as she rubbed the baby-soft fabric against her cheek. How lucky could she get?

Much luckier.

The next day, she'd unearthed Gore-Tex gloves, then snow boots and a hat, followed by another pair of jeans and a cashmere sweater—with a tag from the Gap still attached under the arm.

If she got any "luckier," she'd be Irish.

Dee fingered the cuff of her pink sweater. He really needed to stop with the gifts before her IOU pad over-flowed. She was tempted to sit on her pride awhile longer and see how far Jacob would carry the magical lost-and-found game. Aside from the fact she desper-ately needed the clothes, the tokens had also carried her through a week of disappointments as they uncovered nothing earth-shattering about her identity.

Thanks to Jacob's quizzing, she'd had small break-throughs. She and Jacob often sat in front of the lobby fireplace eating popcorn and flipping through maga-zines to see if any of the pictures prompted a memory. Flashes taunted her, but offered her nothing concrete.

The smell of roses on a corsage pinned to a prom dress.

The wind on her face during a childhood bicycle ride with a friend.

The sound of planes roaring overhead… At a base? During an air show?

Regardless, she couldn't help but notice how often her impressions included something to do with the military lately. Could she be blending her present with Jacob into her past? Or were the memories real? She honestly didn't know.

Sometimes she wondered if she might be fighting herself because the present seemed so appealing. And handsome. And hot. Dee smoothed her hands along the fuzzy softness of her new sweater.

Still, the time had come to put a stop to Jacob's charity.

This didn't seem the best time to approach him, though, with so many people around. Were his friends always so social on the weekends?

His military pals from the diner had apparently spread the word about her because a half dozen had come to check her out. She couldn't keep the names straight, especially when they rarely went by a real name, instead using their call signs such as Picasso and Tag. Crusty and Bronco had both brought their wives and kids—she'd been happy to see Kathleen again.

Jacob had a wide circle of friends and support. She envied him that, even as he wrestled with arranging his life. Her gaze shifted to Emily, who was on the sofa, writing in her journal while the baby slept in her swing.

For once, it wasn't snowing. The sky stretched across a mountainous forever, interrupted only by the occasional airplane from the base rumbling past. Dee rubbed her hands over the goose bumps raising along her skin.

Restlessly, she closed the closet door and parked herself behind the computer. She'd found doing random Google searches sometimes sparked a memory.

Emily shifted on the sofa, Naugahyde crackling. "Guys are kinda dense, don't you think?"

Dee swallowed a laugh. "What brought that up?"

"Oh, just stuff."

"Like?" Dee nodded toward the window.

Outside, Chase helped Jacob salt down sidewalks— when the teen wasn't lobbing snowballs at random targets.

"Well, Chase comes to pick me up last night, and he's so clueless. He doesn't even walk to the door. He just honks the horn. I don't expect him to, like, open doors and pull out chairs and all that stuff, but he could at least ring the bell, don'tcha think?"

"That would be the polite thing to do." Dee swept aside Emily's feet and sat beside her. "Maybe he doesn't know better."

"Have you met his mom?" Emily shot a glare out the window and mumbled, "Or maybe he doesn't want to mess with having a kid."

The baby swing clicked softly.

Life hadn't played fair with the girl, either, Dee thought.

Emily locked her journal and pitched it to the floor. "It's no big deal really. I'll just freeze Chase out for a little while longer until he gets the message."

"Or you could tell him." She couldn't squelch the longing to dispense maternal wisdom about boys and dating.

"Yeah, right." Emily hitched her knees up to her chest and tugged her baggy T-shirt over them. Her face turned moony-eyed with adolescent longing as she stared at Chase.

Was she much better, Dee wondered, watching Jacob, starving for a glimpse of him? He hadn't made a move on her all week. That should have been good, except it gave her too much time to get to know him, really know him across the dinner table.

She liked what she'd found—too much.

Even if she wasn't a married woman, she couldn't afford distractions, not now. And Jacob was a great big, hunkish distraction. "Do you have plans for tonight?"

"The three of us are gonna drive into Tacoma for a movie to celebrate Valentine's Day—if I decide to forgive him."

Valentine's Day? She hadn't even thought to make note of the date; now she couldn't think of anything other than the holiday reserved for lovers.

Emily cast another baleful look at the window. Chase grabbed the shovel at his feet. Jacob launched snowballs baseball-style for the boy to smack.

Could Jacob really be as wonderful as he seemed? Okay, occasionally moody, but wonderful all the same.

Had the father of her child been this great? Did he drive her to distraction with just a look?

Valentine's Day really stunk when a person's love life sucked.

Emily's fingers walked along the sofa back to pick at a crack in the upholstery. "You okay?"

"Huh?" Dee shook herself free of the self-pity. The kid didn't need any more worries than she already had. "Of course. Just feeling lazy today, I guess."

Emily picked at Dee's cuff. "Nice sweater."

"Thanks, it's—" Dee acted on a hunch and continued, "My favorite color. You really did a great job matching up my size."

"Thanks. I figured you were— Hey!"

Dee leaned back, her eyes narrowing. "He sent you shopping, didn't he?"

"Oh, man." Emily slouched into her clothes. "Jacob's gonna kill me for spilling the secret. How did you guess?"

"I can't envision him wandering through racks at the Gap." A laugh slid past Dee's lips, followed by Emily's giggle. "Thank you. But no more charity for me, okay?"

"Hey, there's nothing like shopping on someone else's dime, and you really needed the clothes." Her brows pulled together. "You like everything, don't you?"

"Oh, honey, of course I do— How much more is there?"

A wicked grin crept up the girl's face. "You'll see. Besides, how could I turn him down? He watched Madison and sprung for a supper for Chase and me."

Frustration chugged through Dee. "I don't even want to think of what all of this cost."

"Quit worrying. He's got a steady job and savior complex. It's best to just let him have his way."

Dee could sense more coming and held her silence while the teen pulled her thoughts together. Her computer search could wait. The baby swing clicked away in the silence.

Emily finally sighed. "I guess I'll have to take my own advice and just go live with Jacob." She glanced at Madison. "It's not like I have a lot of choices."

"I'm sorry, sweetie. I wish I had an answer for you." Dee tugged on the hem of her latest charity gift.

Jacob took care of everyone, shoveling driveways, pulling cars out of ditches, even helping finance teenage dates. Three days of cleaning with Grace had clued Dee in that Jacob wasn't paying for much. The woman had cataracts for crying out loud. She couldn't see dust until it flew up her nose.

Emily pegged it, all right. Jacob suffered from a major case of protector syndrome.

Which meant she wasn't anyone special to him, just another stray wandering into his life. She couldn't shrug free of the feeling she wanted to be more.

Problem was, Jacob deserved to have someone who could take care of him, as well. He deserved an equal, not another charity case.

Why did that Jacob Stone have to screw up everything? The man was too damn possessive of her, a female who wanted to haul butt with her child.

His kid.

The Suburban cranked to life. He'd planned everything to a tee, how to shake free of her while keeping his kid close, but now Stone was helping her. Before long, she would be able to stand on her own and that would threaten all of his plans. He needed more time, something that bastard could ruin.

He backed the SUV out of the parking space before pulling onto the highway. Once he cruised to sixty miles per hour, he slid in a CD, cranking the volume so the kid in back would settle down. Shouldn't take too long since he'd already figured out the tyke's favorites.

He would have to wait until his child fell asleep tonight before making a move to regain control. But without question, something needed to happen soon to shake things up.

And what was the best way to get back at a man who didn't scare easily? Hit him where he was vulnerable. Mess with his woman.

Luckily, he had access to Dee's room key.

Sitting in the back of the Ford pickup and watching the stars, Jacob didn't hear Dee's footsteps until she tossed a blanket into the truck bed. He lowered the beer from his mouth. "Get back inside where it's warm."

He winced at his own irritable tone, not that it seemed to deter Dee.

"What are you talking about? It's a balmy forty degrees out here tonight. And no wind chill. The snow's even melting. I barely need a coat." She hooked her knee on the tailgate and hefted herself up. "Mind some company?"

"Yes." He'd had a crap day.

His time with Chase hadn't netted any great reassurance either way. The guy vowed he loved Emily, but acted like more of a playmate with Madison.

Then he'd realized Emily had screwed up the cash drawer again, coming out short.

And to top it off, Dee looked too damn hot in the new

clothes. Helping her was playing hell with his libido. The pink sweater had hugged her breasts all day long.

Just staring at her coat, he wanted to slip his hands beneath and find the soft cashmere—the even softer woman. "Dee, go back inside."

Ignoring him, she closed the last two feet between them, working her way over the slick patches of metal. Parking lot lights hummed in the silence as she stood, unmoving, hands stuffed in her coat pockets.

Somehow he couldn't scavenge the words to make her leave. "Damn, you're stubborn."

"Damn, you're cranky." Without giving him time for a comeback, she jabbed her thumb upward. "Get up."

"What?"

"Get up. I want to spread out the blanket to sit on."

He eased to his feet. Why did she have to invade his space, showing up all hot and smelling good when he just wanted to drink his beer and watch the Northern Lights in peace? "I didn't invite you out here."

"But you have the best seat in the house."

Best seat? She couldn't mean the double entendre the way he would have in referring to her. Still, a grin teased at his face.

Her startled gaze flew to his, down to his backside and up again. A flush crawled up her cheeks that threatened to raise the temperature five degrees. "I, uh, your seat…"

"Thanks."

"Best place to view the Northern Lights, I meant,"

Dee said in a prim, schoolmarm tone. She whipped the blanket out and plopped down. "Come on. Sit."

He recognized a determined woman when he saw one. Arguing would get him nothing but fired up and frustrated—more frustrated. And he didn't really want her to go.

"Here." She flung a wad of something into his lap before dragging a corner of the blanket over her shoulder.

Jacob uncurled one hand from his bottle and picked up...a hat. He set his beer to the side and turned to Dee. "You have a thing about hats."

"Well then, put it on."

"Bossy." A half smile touched his lips, if not his mood. He reached for Dee's scarf. Did she know she swayed toward him anytime he brushed near her? Like now. Slowly, he unwrapped the length from around her ears. Dee listed forward. It would be so easy to cover her mouth with his and lose himself in her softness.

He tugged the stocking cap over her head. "Hat's on."

"Very funny."

Taking more time than he needed, he pulled her hair free from the back, brushed stray strands away from her face. He ached to pitch aside his gloves and warm her skin with his.

The puffs of air coming from her mouth grew faster, heavier. "I meant for you to put it on yourself."

His smile hitched higher. "To quote Emily, 'Duh.'"

He flipped the collar of his coat up and retrieved his

bottle. One long swallow later, he relaxed against the cab of his truck. He wasn't drunk, even though he wanted to be, just buzzed enough to forget why he needed to send Dee back inside. So he let her stay.

How tempting could she be, swaddled in a wool coat with an oversize knit cap on her head? Too tempting after his having spent the day battling his hunger for her. He'd all but gawked through the window at her like some drooling adolescent.

Damn, she was cute.

Jacob tipped the bottle back again.

She pointed into the distance toward the lights striping the sky over the Cascade Range. "That's Mount Rainier, right?"

He nodded. "Yeah, except around here we call it 'The Mountain.'"

She chewed her top lip. "That could be a sign, then, that I'm not from this area."

"Could be. Nice catch on your part. The way you're putting pieces together, it's only a matter of time until you have your memory back." He wanted that for her, even as he wondered how it would affect whatever the hell was drawing them to each other.

"I remembered something. I think my Internet cruising may be working at sparking memories."

The beer turned flat on his tongue. He should be happy for her, and all he could think was, *Now she'll leave sooner.*

"That's great. Tell me about it," he prompted as he'd

done often during their memory-jogging sessions. Except now her voice held an edge that told him this one was about more than a simple prom dress.

"It's not much really. Just a snippet."

"Tell me anyway."

She crossed her legs and canted forward. "I was looking up stuff on Valentine's Day and I came across an article about Valentine's Day getaways."

"Valentine's Day? Oh, hell, that's today isn't it? The holiday for women."

She elbowed him. "For guys, too."

"Yeah, whatever." He grinned, then remembered… "Tell me about your memory." A memory sparked by Cupid would likely be about some other guy. He wished he'd brought a six-pack of beer out with him.

"I'm swimming in an indoor pool, and there are mountains showing through the glass wall, like it's a resort area."

He so didn't want to hear about her romantic getaway with a Mr. Smith. "Uh-huh."

"I wade back toward the stairs, and I'm calling out to someone about not forgetting the baby's water wings."

Hell. He'd been a selfish ass thinking of his own needs when it came to her memory. He'd all but forgotten she had a child in the picture.

She glanced at him, her eyes unblinking. "You know, water wings, those little inflatable things that go around children's arms when they're swimming."

"I know." Over Dee's shoulder, hazy lights streaked

across the sky, as magnificent as ever, but he focused on her.

"Then I hold out my hands for my baby, and man, I'm happy." She tipped her face up, a Madonna glow shimmering from her like the nimbus glow overhead. "I can already feel the weight of that chubby little body settling against my breasts. I can smell baby shampoo and powder. And I reach just a little more…into empty air."

Strain pulled lines into the corners of her eyes. "I can't help but wonder if it might be better remembering nothing. These hints are…torture. I don't even know for sure if the child I'm remembering is mine. Maybe I was helping a friend or even some stranger as I longed for a kid I don't have anymore."

Seeing the pain in her eyes made him want to gather her in his arms and take life's blows for her. Jacob lifted his bottle. "Want some?"

"Yeah," she said through a watery chuckle. "I think I do."

Dee gripped the neck with her thumb and three fingers, pinky extended, and sipped.

She grimaced.

He allowed himself a rusty chuckle. "Guess we can surmise you're not much of a beer drinker."

"You wouldn't happen to have a nice bottle of Merlot on hand would you?"

"Fresh out."

"Too bad."

The curve of her grin enticed him to forget with an intoxication that beat anything waiting for him in a bottle.

Northern Lights continued to shoot their paths, silver and pink fingers of light surging across the sky. He had a beautiful woman beside him on Valentine's Day. It was the perfect setting for seduction—any other night.

Dee scratched a fingernail along the beer label. "Sometimes I wonder if I'm making these memories up, creating a past that I want to have."

"Do you really believe that?"

She glanced at him. "No. But it's easier to accept than thinking about a child going to bed without his or her mother." Her fists clenched. "Damn it, Jacob, why isn't anyone looking for me?"

The frustration in her voice slayed him—and justified his near-savage need to touch her. He wrapped an arm around her shoulders. "I don't know."

Her head fell to rest against his chest. "You would never do it, let someone you care about fade away."

But he'd done just that with his sister.

Jacob shoved the thought aside for the moment and focused on Dee.

She relaxed against him. "When I have these flashes, I know how I felt. Even when I can't see everything, the emotions are so clear." She tilted her face up to his. "I love this child, so it must not be a stranger after all. How can I feel so much for a person I wouldn't even recognize on the street? Is that crazy?"

"Not at all." The warmth of her seared his side, firing a need to pull her closer. But first he had to know. "What about when you're asking for the water-wings? How do you feel about the person you're talking to? What do you hear in response?"

"Airplanes," she blurted, then looked down at the beer bottle between them, still cradled in her hand. "Silly, and not at all helpful."

Abruptly she tipped back the bottle for a long gulp at odds with her pinky waving defiantly in the night. She swiped her wrist across her mouth and passed the beer back to him. "Here, take it before I finish it all."

Their fingers brushed as he reclaimed his drink. He wanted her, wanted to lose himself in her softness, her innocence.

With a last, token effort at distancing himself from Dee, Jacob emptied his longneck with a final swallow. Damn, but he could taste her on the glass. And damned again if he didn't intend to indulge in a fuller sampling of undiluted Dee.

Chapter 9

Dee watched Jacob lower the bottle, his lips still damp from the beer they'd shared. She couldn't look away from his mouth, couldn't stop wanting to kiss him again. But she wouldn't be the one to make the first move, not this time. Parking lot lights shimmered with a muted glow while she waited, thirsty for the taste of Jacob.

Reaching past her, he set aside the longneck. His arm brushed hers, the heat of his chest warming her until her breasts tightened in response beneath her coat. His eyes stilled her and embraced her with a stormy blue desire, an ache mirrored inside her.

She could see he needed her, maybe for all the wrong

reasons, just as she'd needed him after the doctor visit. Suddenly what should be wrong felt incredibly right.

She swayed forward.

"Ah, Dee." He groaned her name, low and husky, more beautiful coming from his mouth than a simple syllable should have any right to be.

His hand shot up to cup the back of her head, tuck under the hat and flick it free. Her hair swirled around her as his fingers combed sensuous paths along her scalp.

Endless seconds later, Jacob's mouth skimmed hers. Relief swelled through her as she nestled where she'd burned to be all day, all week, for as long as she could remember. He claimed her mouth. Claimed, and demanded she do the same in return. He tugged on her bottom lip, enticed until she opened to accept him.

Dee decided she'd acquired a taste for beer after all, or maybe it was the way the rich ferment tasted on Jacob's tongue. The warm tang of it induced a heady rush. Surely the buzzing along her every nerve was a by-product of alcohol.

Yeah, right.

Locking her arms around Jacob's neck, she explored the breadth of his shoulders as his restless hands slipped beneath her coat to her back, down her waist. God he was big, yet no longer intimidating as she'd feared the first time her eyes traveled up the length of him. She'd learned he used his size for protection rather than intimidation.

Dee snuggled closer, couldn't get close enough. Without breaking their kiss, Jacob lowered her to the quilt and blanketed her with his body as their legs tangled. Dee danced her tongue against his, learning the taste of Jacob, which only served to send her into another dizzying spiral of pure sensation.

They rolled until she landed on top, and she found she liked it there. Jacob shifted to take her weight fully upon him. She liked that even more, Jacob allowing her some control for a change, even in such a fundamental way.

A clatter rumbled along the truck bed. Dee tried to block out what she didn't want to hear. The beer bottle clanked, spinning until it shattered against the icy parking lot.

"Jacob—"

"I'll clean it up later." He nuzzled her neck again, but the moment had been broken, as well.

Realization chilled Dee more than the frost in the air. What was she doing? Not five minutes ago she'd been sharing memories of the family she'd most likely left behind, and now she was crawling all over Jacob like some sex-starved teenager because of Valentine's Day sentimentality.

Dee pushed herself up beside him. Jacob blinked twice before flinging his arm over his face.

His arm fell away. "I'm s—"

"Don't say you're sorry." She hugged her knees to her chest in counterpressure against an ache with Jacob's name tattooed all over it. "I'm the one who should apologize."

Jacob jackknifed up as he raked his hands through his hair. It wasn't long hair, but she'd managed to make a fine mess of it all the same, just like she'd done with her life. And might do with his if she wasn't careful.

"What is it with me, Jacob? I told myself it didn't matter what had happened before, only what I do now, but I can't even keep my hands off you for a week. I barely know anything about you, like your favorite ice cream or why your friends call you Mako." She squeezed her knees harder, pushing all the air free until she could only whisper, "What kind of a woman am I?"

He grasped her chin, his grip a fraction past gentle. "I don't know what the hell was going on in your life before you came here, either. But regardless of how long we've spent together, I *do* know who you are, the person that's real, underneath any layer of memories." His touch gentled to a caress. "There's an innocence and goodness in you that's rare, special. Don't doubt it for a minute."

She wanted to believe him, yearned to grasp his words with both hands and accept them simply because Jacob said so. But that kind of blind faith, a dependency, also raked over an innately pragmatic part of her.

She had to prove to herself she wasn't simply a "Mrs. Smith" who drooled over any man. "Then why do I want to lie back on that blanket and finish this?"

Jacob's jaw flexed.

Dee's shivered in response. "Not smart, huh?"

"Nope." His hand shook as he hooked her hair

behind her ear. A lone trailer of the Northern Lights shimmered across the sky. "I think you should go inside now."

"Right. Of course." She scrambled toward the tailgate. "Dee?"

She glanced over her shoulder. Heaven help her if he called her back. "Yes?"

"Butter pecan ice cream. And Mako started out as Maaco, like the auto repair company, because I can fix any engine on any vehicle. Later the spelling tweaked to Mako, as in the shark, because it sounds cool." He tipped back his head, eyes tipped toward the stars, conversation over.

His words settled into her memory along with his assertion that he knew her very well, regardless of time. She wanted... She didn't know what.

A final look at Jacob confirmed he'd withdrawn from her. How remote he seemed, with those shadows muting the vibrancy of his beautiful eyes like the aurora lighting the sky then slipping away leaving the world feeling colder and darker than before.

In spite of all her intentions to be his friend while she pieced her life together, she'd done it again. She'd thrown herself at him. It didn't matter that he'd made the first move tonight. She hadn't thought to push him away for a long time.

Still wished she hadn't pushed him away at all.

Dee scrambled out of the truck and raced as fast as she dared through the sludge back toward the warm safety and stark isolation of her hotel room.

* * *

Dee sank deeper into the soothing bubble bath, then jolted as she realized the water had cooled. How long had she been in here since tearing off her clothes to soak after the frustrating encounter with Jacob in his truck?

She swiped at the remaining few frothy patches of soap. She must have drifted off. Too bad she couldn't wake up and find this whole time had been some freaky nightmare.

Except she wouldn't want to wish away Jacob.

How many of her feelings for him were tied up in dependence? Or some sort of weird crush because he'd saved her? She wanted to think she was above such shallowness, but she didn't really know that much about herself.

She did, however, know everything about Jacob so far spoke of honor and goodness. Her attraction to him was based on more than the way he filled out his blue jeans.

Laughing, she blew bubbles from the back of her hand. Laughter echoed in the small bathroom, bouncing off the tile and back around her until silence fell again.

Nothing but *drip, drip, drip* from the faucet.

An eerie sensation slid over her, chilling her faster than the cooling water. She tried to get a grip. Of course it was quiet. She was alone in her room, but she'd locked the door.

Had she put on the chain and the dead bolt?

She couldn't remember. How could she have grown so complacent in such a short time? She shouldn't count on others for her safety. No matter how much help Jacob and his friends offered, they had only known her a short while. How important could she really be to them so fast? She wanted to start relying on herself, to grow stronger to face whatever life she'd forgotten.

Carefully, she rose from the tub and reached for a towel to wrap around herself. Not much for armor, but she was only confronting ghostly fears, nothing real except her paranoia.

A bracing breath later, she twisted the doorknob and stepped into the room to—

Nobody. The motel room was empty but for the two neatly made-up beds and a chair with her hand-me-down blue robe on the armrest. She sagged back against the sink in the dressing area with relief.

Turning, she reached for her comb and blinked.

Streaks of bloodred lipstick glared back at her from the mirror. All capital letters. One word.

DEAD.

Jacob tipped back the chair behind the check-in desk and thought about his dead father, really thought about the old man for the first time. He'd done a good job of ignoring the man's presence stamped all over the place, but then Dee had asked about the "Mako" call sign, which led to thoughts of learning everything he could about engines in hopes of earning his father's approval.

Clyde Stone was gone. Really gone. For so many

years, Jacob had worked to gain his dad's attention, then worked harder to ignore the selfish bastard's existence.

Now he was dead and Jacob couldn't stop thinking about him. Because of Dee. Because he realized having a past, even a crummy one, was better than none at all.

They hadn't had much of a father/son relationship, yet the man had been a towering presence. His father put on such a good face, all smiles and laughter—as long as no demands were placed on him. No wonder Clyde had never gone out of his way to make this business a success. He hadn't wanted the commitment.

The last thought stopped him cold.

Had he picked up that very trait from his old man? Sure, thirty-two wasn't old to be a bachelor. However, he couldn't ignore the fact that he usually bailed from any relationship once it grew serious.

He tipped back his beer and stared through the window at the old truck Emily drove. The vehicle should have long ago been sent to the junkyard. No question it would die soon now that their father wasn't around to milk more life out of it. They'd spent a lot of hours tinkering with that engine when Jacob had been a teen.

Those silent moments seeped into his brain—

A muffled noise jerked him back into the moment, the sound of a door opening outside, crashing against the wall.

Jacob vaulted to his feet and crossed to the wide window, peering farther down the parking lot. Holy crap. Dee bolted out to the walkway wearing just a robe and untied tennis shoes. Her wet hair rode the wind behind her as she raced toward the office.

What the hell was going on?

He threw open the door and caught her as she slipped on the steps. "Dee? What's wrong?"

Had she suddenly remembered? She definitely looked stunned.

"Someone br-broke into my r-room." Her teeth chattered, with cold or fear or both.

He could certainly understand because right now he felt chilled to the bone. "Are you okay?"

While hauling her into the office, he searched the parking lot for signs of an intruder. He saw plenty of tire ruts and recalled hearing minimal traffic while he'd sat in his truck, but nothing now.

And hell, he needed to get to Emily and the baby.

"I'm f-fine. Whoever it was left before I got out of the tub."

"Good. Good." He pointed to a connecting door. "Go through there, stay with Emily and call the police while I check outside."

She gripped his arm. "Be careful. Please."

"Of course," he responded automatically, already focused on the parking lot and looking for whoever had dared threaten Dee.

Chapter 10

No one was looking for her. Dee had to accept it.

She spread her arms to pull the towel taut before folding it. Grace silently folded a second pile while the dryer tumbled a fresh load in the motel laundry room.

Three days had passed since someone had broken in and written *DEAD* on her mirror. Not that Jacob had been able to find anyone. Not that the cops had uncovered anything further.

Other than noting the lipstick tube had been completely wiped clean of prints.

She'd told them the lipstick hadn't been there before, but she could tell they thought she'd absentmindedly forgotten. She disagreed then and now. She might not know some things about herself, but she knew for darn sure she hadn't left out a lipstick tube since she'd taken a careful inventory of her meager possessions after waking up with nothing but a hundred dollars and an EpiPen. She didn't have a stitch of makeup to her name.

Dee reminded herself to be grateful for what she did have. People seemed to accept her in spite of the amnesia.

At least there were people here who cared enough to notice if she fell off the face of the earth again. Grace, Emily…and Jacob.

Dee clutched the towel to her belly in counterpressure against the ache that had only increased since their kiss in the truck. An ache she couldn't fill. Soon, he would be returning to his Charleston base.

Since she'd landed in Rockfish, the police hadn't unearthed so much as a nibble on her identity, much less help in finding a child she wasn't sure she still had. Even a long-shot attempt at hypnosis had been a bust. She and Jacob had garnered more success unearthing memories through simple brainstorming conversations. At times, she felt a change in herself, as if her mind were pregnant with memories, ready to give birth to them. And then nothing…

Her few memories of her child were real, of that she had no doubt. As days passed, she had to explore the possibility that she'd given up her baby, or that, heaven forbid, it had died. Had she lost her child *and* a husband,

and that was why she had no one left to notice her absence? Reluctantly, her mind traveled that painful path.

Perhaps in her grief she had lost herself in shallow encounters with men like Mr. Smith. Certainly such all-encompassing pain could make a person want to forget. The scenario, while excruciating, made sense.

Otherwise, wouldn't she be needed enough for someone to look for her? How devastating to think her life mattered so little that she could disappear.

She had to find answers. The lack of control threatened to drive her crazy. All she could do was continue to try, pester the police and save money for a private investigator.

Meanwhile, how could she be true to an unknown past while taking a chance on the future before Jacob left?

Standing outside the lobby closet, Jacob stuffed his military-issue snow parka into his gear bag. As always, the prospect of helping with a Civil Air Patrol search and rescue mission charged him, reminding him of his Air Force job waiting for him.

Only four days remained before he had to return to Charleston and he still hadn't settled anything with Emily. His sister was going to have to accept the fact that she had to go with him. Starting tomorrow, they would have to get her school records, begin packing, hire someone to manage the motel...

Jacob glanced at Dee as she typed on the computer at the registration desk. "I can't wait for Chase any longer.

If he shows, let him know I've left to hook up with Bronco and Tag. He can meet us at McChord. He'll have at least a half-hour window before the ground team heads out to start sweeping the area for the missing plane."

Dee spun in the chair to face him, her hair swinging to drape around her shoulders. "No problem. I'll pass along the message."

Tearing himself away from the power of Dee's honey-brown eyes, Jacob stuffed a box of packaged MREs—meals ready to eat—on top of his winter gear. "Are you sure you'll be okay here alone? I could be gone all night."

With two incidents of missing money from the drawer still unsolved, he worried about leaving her alone, unprotected. The cops hadn't learned anything more about the intruder. He'd added extra security lights with motion sensors outside. He'd also given Dee a cell phone to carry with her at all times—in spite of her protests of "no charity."

"I'll be fine." She stood and perched her hip against the counter, a shapely hip cupped by well-washed denim. "I can handle the phone lines for a few hours without you or Emily for backup."

His hands itched. They begged him to fit both palms along those hips and pull her toward him. She'd started a thaw inside him that night in the back of the pickup. Her daily presence and that face-life-head-on attitude had ended his solitary days. A primal male part of him urged Jacob to pursue her, consequences be damned, before some other man came back to claim her.

What would he do then? It wasn't as if he was any good at long-term. While he might not know much about Dee Smith, any fool could see she was the minivan-and-cookies type. His future mapped out more along the lines of wandering the world—anywhere but Rockfish with all its memories. Even moving to Tacoma shouted at revisiting the place he'd worked so damn hard to leave.

But she sure did look good in those jeans, and at his dinner table—and in his life. He'd been considering moving back here for Emily anyway, past be damned. Maybe Dee and Grace could run the motel for the few months until he managed the transfer and then...

"Jacob? Are you okay?"

"Yeah." He cleared his throat so he could push free a full sentence. "This counts as overtime, you know."

"This counts as doing a favor for a friend."

Slowly he zipped the bag to give himself time to think before looking at Dee. "Is that what we are, friends?"

She fingered the cuff of her yellow flowered shirt, the flannel one he'd sent Emily to buy on her first shopping trip. The color turned Dee's skin the prettiest creamy shade, like fine china he wanted to hold but worried he might break.

"I'd like to think so." She leaned forward across the counter. "Let me do this for you. Please."

He'd become accustomed to having her around, sometimes finding himself surprised at how many ways she'd sashayed her gently curved body and bossy ways into his motel and into his every thought.

And his life was better for it.

A knot held tight in his chest uncoiled, relaxed. "Okay."

"Okay? Really? No overtime?"

"No overtime. And thanks." Jacob hefted his bag and started toward the door.

"Jacob?"

He glanced back over his shoulder. "What?"

"I don't want overtime."

"I heard you."

"But you could take me out to eat."

Damn, but she'd thrown him another curve. *Curves.* Of its own volition, his gaze flowed over her. *Curves.* He needed to erase that word from his vocabulary.

How could one woman bring such mayhem and peace at the same time? She scared the hell out of him. Given the look on her face, he suspected she'd just scared the hell out of herself, as well. "Just friends going to the diner?"

They'd hidden out at the diner more than once when the prospect of all those motel beds waiting to be used had overpowered them.

She shrugged, but didn't agree. He looked deeper in her eyes and saw exactly what he'd feared—and hoped—to find over the past few days. They were becoming more than friends. He wanted this woman to be more than his friend. He wanted to be her lover.

How many more empty police reports would it take before he could act on that? His body jolted in response at the mere thought.

Not five seconds ago he'd told himself he wasn't right for her—regardless.

Well, dinner wasn't a raging affair.

He could take her to supper. They'd eaten together every night like some old married couple, except without dessert sex.

Jacob stifled a groan.

Dee ducked her head and picked at her cuff again. "Never mind. Forget I said it. You don't owe me for helping out. If anything, I owe you. Watching the desk for a few hours won't even put a dent in my debt."

There were those soulful, hurt eyes again, stabbing right through him. He didn't stand a chance. "We could hunt down a restaurant in Tacoma that would serve you a bottle of Merlot."

The invitation fell out of Jacob's mouth before he could give himself time to think. And regret.

She tipped her chin with that Dee spirit he'd come to admire. She recovered quickly, he'd grant her that.

Dee pulled free a McChord base newspaper from beside the computer and plopped it on the counter. She pointed to an ad. "Or we could go to the base and have dinner at the NCO Club."

Jacob walked toward her, slowly, and traced a finger along the edges of the paper. A paper that had been neatly folded to the page in advance, as if she'd been planning this. Another curve. "You'd like to go to the NCO Club?"

He'd noticed how often she flinched when the military airplanes flew overhead, how she went quiet whenever friends from the base showed up. Had the man who fathered her child been in the service?

"I can honestly say I can't recall ever having been to one before," she rambled nervously, her cheeks pinkening to match the flowers on her shirt. "I'm sure they have Merlot there. We can save Tacoma for another night."

Another night. Another date. But not a date. Surely spending his last few evenings away from the intimacy of the motel would be wise.

He ignored the niggling sense that he was deluding himself and making a mistake, a big one. They were about to take a step forward that couldn't be backtracked if the bottom fell out later. "All right then. Dinner at the base."

Dee smiled, another curve of hers he'd come to enjoy viewing.

Just a simple night away from the Lodge, Jacob reminded himself.

He backed up a step. "Give Chase's mom a call if he doesn't show soon."

"I will. And, Jacob?"

"Yeah?"

"Be careful."

Jacob nodded and bolted out the door, wondering how a tiny scrap of a woman had him on the run when he'd faced down enemy threats twice her size.

Dee settled in for a slow night. No tour buses were scheduled, and the weather forecast would deter most impulsive travelers. Which left her with all night to think about what she'd asked Jacob.

Man, she had the munchies.

The vending machines called to her. At least she could feed one hunger without risking more than a couple of extra pounds. She scrounged in her pockets for loose change. After coming up with nothing but two quarters, she hit pay dirt with a one-dollar bill.

She still couldn't believe she'd actually asked Jacob out, not that it qualified as a date, really. Just a friendly evening out. A nice, safe step toward starting a new life for herself. She didn't plan to give up on the old one, but it could be years before she remembered. Meanwhile, she needed to create a life for herself outside the constant wondering and worrying, or she truly would lose her mind. Then she would be of no use to her child or herself.

After she'd bought a bag of sour cream and onion chips, Dee fed the dollar into the soda machine. It disappeared...and rolled back out. She flattened the bill and tried again.

No luck.

A quick trip to the cash drawer built in under the counter left her with change in hand for another try.

The red Sold Out light glared on both Coke buttons. Dee sighed. She really wanted a Coke. She could always raid Jacob's kitchen and pay him back later. Heaven knew he'd extended the offer often enough when she'd helped at the desk before.

As she snagged a can from his refrigerator, Dee heard the front door to the lobby blast open. She swallowed a sip and hollered, "Hold on a minute. I'll be right out."

Dee nudged the refrigerator door shut with her hip. In the lobby, she found Chase hovering behind the counter. "Sorry, Chase, but they had to go on without you. Jacob said for you to meet them at the base. If you leave now, you can probably make it before the ground crew heads out."

"Oh, yeah, sure." He jammed his hands in his pockets, his baggy camouflage pants riding low from the extra pressure.

She waited, but he didn't move. "They're only about ten minutes ahead of you. Maybe you can call on the cell phone and ask them to wait."

"I'll just skip this one."

Dee chewed her lip to keep from dishing out a lesson on following through with responsibilities. "You could hang out with Emily. I think Madison is already asleep."

Chase shuffled from foot to foot. "Nah, no need. I'll just hit the road."

Her bottom lip was getting a real workout tonight. Rather than argue with Chase, she decided to phone his mother after he left. "Good night, then."

"'Night." He brushed past, his hip bumping the half-open cash register drawer.

Dee stared at the drawer, trying to deny what she knew to be true. She'd closed it after making change.

She wouldn't have been so careless as to leave the drawer hanging open.

Chase couldn't have possibly… She cast a furtive glance at the teen crossing to the door.

Instinct told her he most certainly had.

Popping open the drawer the rest of the way, she looked inside. The slot that should have held a stack of twenties now contained a lone bill, as if someone hadn't wanted to be so obvious as to empty out the space. "Hey, Chase. Hold on a sec."

His jerky look back over his shoulder, the defensive glint in his eyes, confirmed her fears. He'd lifted money from the cash register.

Jacob would be livid. Hell, she was livid. She couldn't even bear to consider what this meant for Emily and Madison.

She reacted with her heart rather than her head, wanting to save Jacob from knowing. "Put the money back, Chase, and we can let this go."

With a snap of his head, he flicked a hank of walnut hair from his face. The defensive glint evaporated, a belligerent glare taking its place. "What money?"

"I'm not stupid, so don't act like I am. Put it back."

Chase sauntered forward. Smugness mushroomed from his every step like an insidious threat. "Even if there was money missing, how's Jacob gonna know you didn't take it?"

He stopped almost toe-to-toe with her. The lobby suddenly seemed small…and deserted. Wind moaned through the eaves while Dee struggled not to flinch. How could she and Jacob both have misjudged this kid?

Chase didn't look much like a kid at the moment.

The phone shrieked through the silence. They both twitched, but Chase didn't budge.

"Fine, Chase. We'll play this your way." She pivoted away to dismiss him, cowardly, maybe, but she wanted him out of the lobby. Now. She reached for the phone.

His hand fell on her shoulder. Dee's stomach lurched as if she'd taken a wrong turn off a mountain curve.

Show no fear. Regardless of how he looked he was just a kid. Pull out the adult authority, put him in his place and get him out the door.

Dee plastered her best "schoolmarm frown" in place and shrugged his hand loose. "Chase, step back."

His bravado slipped. Dee almost sagged with relief—until his eyes narrowed with a male arrogance meant to intimidate, insult.

The phone stopped ringing.

Where was the child who'd swung a shovel at snowballs? The boy who'd chased his girlfriend through the snow, the young man who held his baby tenderly?

Chase ambled forward, forcing her to retreat until the backs of her legs pressed against the computer chair. He smiled, but it wasn't pleasant or in any way childish. "You have quite a rep around here thanks to all the gossip. No secrets in this town. People aren't sure what to think of your whacky amnesia claim. You're not in any position to be talking trash about me."

His eyes journeyed a slow drag down her body and back up again, lingering on strategic places.

A shiver trickled down Dee's spine like a melting icicle. Without another word, she pushed past him. Maybe she could lock herself in Jacob's apartment. Chase's hand snaked out. He grabbed her shirtfront.

"Not so fast." He twisted the fabric, yanking her forward. "Where do you think you're going?"

The chill iced all the way through her veins.

Where do you think you're going?

His words echoed in her head, deeper pitched.

Where do you think you're going?

A Midwestern twang sounded, rather than Chase's local lilt.

Fear gripped her tighter than Chase's fist on her shirt. Dee's feet tangled. The shirt pulled taut. Panic frothed, higher, higher still, until she screamed. Couldn't stop screaming. "No!"

"Calm down." Chase eyed her warily. His hold on her still unrelenting, he shook her. "Don't get wigged out or anything. Hey now—"

—*not so fast,* growled the Midwesterner's voice, a voice from her past.

Dee jerked. Buttons popped from her shirt. She backed away, her steps clumsy and haphazard, until she slammed against the soda machine. Her teeth jarred. She slithered to the floor and huddled, teeth chattering.

In her mind, other buttons popped loose. Coat buttons. She swallowed back the nausea and watched pearl buttons spiral across the tile until they blurred into larger, black buttons from her coat.

You're not going anywhere with my kid. I'll kill him before I let you see him again, Deirdre.

Pain slashed behind her eyes like a needle piercing her skin. White-hot, then frighteningly cold, like a deep sleep or even death. Through the pain emerged a suffocating gush of memories.

She remembered her name.

She remembered her child. Her son.

Both of which might have been cause for rejoicing. Except nausea choked her as, God help her, she remembered her husband.

Chapter 11

Jacob tapped his thumb on the steering wheel, eager to return to the Lodge, to Dee.

The rescue operation had been canceled fifteen minutes out of Rockfish. The missing plane had simply been diverted because of weather. The pilot hadn't closed out his flight plan, and the alert had gone up. Of course, ninety percent of all missing aircraft ended in the same sort of scenario, so Jacob wasn't surprised. Just mildly annoyed at the waste of Civil Air Patrol time.

And the lost evening with Dee, a chance to explore whatever had started changing between them.

The urge to see her crept over him. A quick call to

the Lodge to find Chase wouldn't be out of line. Jacob pulled his cell phone from his back pocket and punched in the number. Five rings later, he disconnected. Why wasn't Dee picking up? Could things be that swamped?

He stared ahead at the approaching lodge and the lot looked sparse as usual. Jacob slowed, headlights sweeping ahead as he pulled in beside Chase's vehicle. Emily would be glad for the extra time together. Jacob looked into the lobby, but didn't see Dee behind the desk.

Hmm... Odd. He opened the truck door.

A muffled scream filtered through the Lodge window. Followed by another. Then unending pain-filled cries.

Dee. Dread coldcocked him just before old instincts rammed into overdrive.

His boots slammed to the icy pavement at a dead run. He skidded toward the motel office. A couple of doors down, Emily poked her head out of her suite of rooms.

He vaulted up the steps two at a time, through the door and came chest-to-chest with Chase, who was leaving. "Chase? What's going on?"

Jacob didn't wait for the answer as he sidestepped to find Dee. Her screams dwindled to a low whimper. She sat with her back against the soda machine, her arms locked around her knees, hands fisted so tightly they trembled. Her eyes stared wide and unfocused.

"Dee?"

She fell silent, gasping big hiccuping breaths. Footsteps filled the silence. Chase shuffled his feet. Emily skidded to a halt in the doorway. Jacob motioned silently for her to stay back.

He approached Dee warily. She'd never looked so fragile, not even when the wind had swept her into the lobby for the first time.

Why had he ever left her alone? "Chase, what the hell's going on?"

"I don't know, man. She just freaked out." Chase backed toward the door until he bumped into Emily, still waiting on the threshold. Jaw slack, she gawked at Dee.

Jacob knelt beside her. He wanted to haul her into his arms and reassure himself she hadn't been hurt. Not the smartest move at the moment.

Go easy. "Dee, honey. Talk. You're scaring me."

She turned those wide, wounded eyes to him, but didn't seem to see him. Never once had he seen her lose it, not when she had a truckload of reasons for turning into a basket case. Something bad must have gone down. Suddenly he wasn't too steady, either.

"It's okay. Just breathe." Jacob stroked her hair, then tucked a knuckle under her chin. His hand bumped her fist—her fist clutching her torn shirt closed. Buttons littered the floor around her.

An opaque curtain of denial fogged Jacob's mind. No way. He couldn't be seeing what he thought. But Chase had been running away from Dee, not toward her.

Jacob scooped a button from the tile. "Chase?"

The lanky teen glanced from the button, to Dee's blouse and back to Jacob. Chase's eyes widened. "Uh-

uh. Not a chance. It's not what you think. She flipped out, just the way I said. I tried to keep her from going outside without a coat. That's how her shirt got ripped."

"Then why were you running away when I got here?"

Chase hesitated. "Uh, I saw you drive up."

Jacob wanted to believe him, but his instincts clamored that Chase wasn't telling everything—shuffling feet, refusal to make eye contact, all the typical signs of lying. Jacob's jaw clenched. He didn't want to wrap his mind around the possibility that Chase had assaulted Dee, or even tried.

A glance at Dee told him she was still out of it. He needed answers from Chase before he could help her. Jacob pinned Chase with an interrogator's gaze and continued smoothing a hand along Dee's hair. "Be straight with me now, or you can talk to the police."

Emily gasped, stepping forward. Jacob kept his eyes on Chase but directed his words toward his sister. "Emily, go back to your room and take care of Madison."

Out of the corner of his eye, he saw her wave the nursery monitor but didn't advance deeper inside.

"Police?" Chase eyed the door hungrily. "I didn't do anything to her. She's just acting or something. Come on, man, you know me. Who's she, anyway, huh? Just some nutcase claiming she has amnesia."

"Enough." Jacob sliced the air with his hand. "Last chance, Chase. The truth."

"Okay." The teen fidgeted, gulped, tugged at his

sagging pants and gulped again. "I hate to tell you this, but when I got here, I found her taking a stack of money out of your cash drawer."

Jacob's hand stilled. His mind turned white-hot. For all of two seconds. Then reason kicked in. Dee wouldn't steal from him. He wished he could attribute the surety to trust, but logic had saved him from the test. If cleaning him out had been her plan, she could have done so a hundred times over. She was the type who turned over pocket change found in linens while cleaning.

But what about Chase? Jacob could see it in the boy's eyes, and the realization made him sick for Emily. He resumed stroking Dee's hair while he studied the signs of guilt stamped all over Chase.

The kid had stolen from him. Jacob swallowed the bilious sting of disappointment. "Empty your pockets."

"What?"

"Jacob?" Emily sidled toward Chase. "You can't really think—"

"Now, Chase." A cool core of certainty congealed in him. "If I'm wrong, I'll apologize. But I'm going to get her side of the story as soon as she calms down."

Chase eyed the door again.

Emily gripped the arm of Chase's jacket. "Prove him wrong. Please."

Chase shrugged free. He jammed his hand into his pocket and whipped out a stack of folded twenty-dollar bills. He didn't even bother making excuses.

"No, Chase." Emily's chin quivered as the nursery monitor hummed in her hand.

"Fine." Chase slammed the wad of cash on the counter. "I didn't walk out of here with it, so there's not a damned thing you can do to me."

Jacob stared at the money and focused on the feel of Dee's hair beneath his hand. When would the anger hit him? Logic told him that's how he should feel. Instead he'd gone numb. Probably for the best, since he had to take care of the mess with Chase and deal with Dee. "Sit down, Chase."

"No way, I'm—"

"Sit," Jacob snapped.

Chase dropped onto the sofa. What had Emily seen in this guy? An escape from Clyde? Or more likely choosing Chase because he was surely the sort who would tweak the old man's nose at every turn.

Jacob relaxed his jaw, lowered his tensed shoulders and regained control. He needed to distance himself from everything, all of them. Emotions clouded judgment.

He turned his attention back to Dee and cupped her face in his hands without allowing himself to savor the softness of her skin. "Snap out of it, Dee. You need to talk to me, or we're heading to the hospital."

Her eyes widened, then cleared. "Jacob?"

"Yeah, Dee." Relief taunted him, so close. "Are you okay? Are you…hurt?"

"I remember everything." Her eyes deepened, darkened, assumed a different quality.

The look of a different woman. The real Dee.

Dee? Hell, he didn't even know her name.

But she'd remembered. He should be happy. He'd worked with her for this moment, yet somehow wasn't ready. Maybe because he knew this was it. Now she would leave.

His hands slid from her face as he let her go. "Tell me."

"I remember my child…and my husband. He took my son, Jacob. He stole my baby."

Deirdre fingered her "Dee" necklace as she waited for the county police. She'd never so much as logged a speeding ticket in her life, yet lately she'd talked to the cops on a regular basis like some criminal. Like her husband. Thanks to her husband.

The metal chilled in her hand. Her son had given her the necklace for Christmas. He'd bought it at a preschool Santa's Gift Shop for students to choose gifts for parents.

Memories she'd chased so vigilantly hurt. Even the beautiful ones stung because of all she'd lost.

Jacob stepped into the lobby, leaving Emily and Chase in the next room—silent—with the door open, waiting to make their statements when the police arrived. Dee didn't care if Jacob pressed charges for her sake, but she didn't blame him for drawing the line at stealing. Chase had been trusted here.

He tossed her a blue Air Force sweatshirt.

"Thank you." At least she could quit worrying about

clutching her buttonless blouse closed. Still she mourned the loss of her pretty flowered shirt, her first gift from Jacob.

As she tugged the sweatshirt over her head, Jacob's scent, his warmth, enveloped her, tempting her to seek the real thing. She had to face the world on her own sometime. Dee whipped her hair free of neckline and took what consolation she could from the generous folds of cotton fleece.

Why wouldn't he step away from the counter and sit by her, comfort her in that sturdy way of his? In a flash of insight she understood. Because he didn't know her anymore. While she didn't feel any different, Jacob saw a stranger.

It was a night full of losses. So she introduced herself to this man she'd known just under two weeks, a lifetime in itself for Dee Smith.

"My name is Deirdre Lambert. I'm from Reno, Nevada." How strange to say that after not knowing so long. How could she ever have forgotten? She hadn't. It had been stolen from her as surely as Chase had taken that money. As the man she'd married had stolen her child.

Humiliation swamped her as she forced herself to tell Jacob the rest. "The Mr. Smith who checked me in was my husband—"

Jacob's fists clenched, the first visible reaction she'd seen from him since Chase had slapped the money on the counter. Could it be jealousy? What should have given her a tiny rush merely saddened her. They'd found the attraction tough enough before, and now her life had snarled into a bigger tangle.

"My *ex*-husband." She threaded her fingers through her hair and mashed the heels of her hands against her temples. "Maybe I'd better back up. There are just so many images crowding my brain, so many thoughts and memories and moments to relive. I feel like I'm in sensory overload."

Dee slumped back on the sofa. Still Jacob stood, unmoving. Maybe it was better they didn't touch. She might shatter like a brittle icicle.

"Blane, my ex-husband, worked for a company that manufactured airplane parts." She tucked her knees up under the overlong sweatshirt as if to insulate herself with Jacob's innate strength. "His partner was convicted of knowingly selling substandard parts to companies under contract to build military aircraft. After coming across some papers in our old files, I started to suspect Blane might have been involved, too."

Now she understood why she winced every time anything military crossed her path. She feared for the people who could be in danger. She couldn't shake the shame over not having somehow known and stopped her husband.

Finally Jacob pushed away from the counter to sit beside her. "And that's when you left him?"

"Actually we divorced a year ago." Blane had been cheating on her with a woman at work.

Dee wondered now how she'd missed the signs for so long. She cringed to think of how she, too, had been caught up in the seeming security of materialism in those days. She wanted much simpler things for herself and her son now.

Jacob's warm body waited inches away, but his gaze stayed focused on the picture of Mount Rainier over the fireplace. Not that she could accept any sympathy from him. He demanded such perfection from himself, how could he ever understand, much less condone how badly she'd screwed up?

"I found out he'd been cheating on me, not some fling even, but a long-term relationship." So much for pride. Blane had trounced hers like grapes in a wine vat, and the product had been beyond bitter.

"I'm sorry." Jacob transferred his gaze to his hands clasped loosely between his knees.

"Blane didn't contest the divorce. I obviously didn't mean that much to him, but he wanted sole custody of our son."

Losing Evan was beyond bearing. She certainly understood that all too well. "I fought him and we ended up with shared custody. Once I found out about his illegal dealings, I got scared for Evan. I knew I didn't have any choice but to go to the police. I was only a day away from turning him in." She started shaking again. "Somehow he must have figured out—from my expression, or maybe I wasn't as subtle in probing for information as I thought."

Jacob's face hardened. "He decided to shut you up."

She nodded, still hardly able to grasp that he would

hurt her deliberately. Believing he could be capable of stealing had torn a hole in her heart. Discovering he could actually try to kill her… She could still hardly grasp what had happened. The ultimate betrayal by a man she'd once thought she loved. "Blane came by my condo, calm as ever. He had something for Evan in the Suburban, a present for Evan's fourth birthday since Blane would be traveling for work."

Her mind flashed with so many kaleidoscope memories. Evan clutching his favorite blanket with quilted airplane squares, the edges now ragged. Blane's earnest blue eyes, so like Evan's.

How could the father of her precious baby boy be totally bad? Surely his love for Evan was one pure part left in Blane, a symbol of what had been good in their marriage. "A little voice deep inside me whispered that he was up to something, but Evan wanted his toy and Blane. I needed to believe there was something honest left inside him. Do you know what I mean?"

"Like wanting to believe Chase could be there for Emily." Jacob's eyes warmed as he finally seemed to see her. "Yeah, Dee…Deirdre. I understand."

Deirdre. Not Dee.

Those last four inches might as well have been a mile. She wanted his arms around her as she shared the most painful part, his strong arms, rather than a sweatshirt substitute.

Damn her pride, she couldn't make herself ask. "He forced me into the Suburban and started driving north, stopping here our first night on the road." She shuddered to think of the red dress he'd made her wear in one of his twisted mind games. "We left early the next morning before dawn, and I was afraid he might make it to Canada. I tried to plan how to get help from the border patrol—then the snowstorm started and Blane made his move. He tossed me out of the car on an abandoned road."

I'll kill him before I let you see him again, Deirdre.

The horror, the fear, the utter helplessness choked her, fresh as if it had happened only moments before. "I hit my head, I think. I must have. Mostly I remember fighting to get to my feet as he drove away with my child."

Jacob reached to stroke her hair. She ducked, too raw, too vulnerable to accept the comfort that would send her crying into his arms.

She had to hold it together, depend on herself and start the search for her child. The search for a trail nearly two weeks cold. "The next thing I remember is stumbling to my feet, confused. I shoved my hands into my coat pockets to warm them and found the hotel key and a hundred dollars. I could only think of getting back here to my baby. Which doesn't make sense because they were already leaving."

"You'd been injured and traumatized. You're lucky you survived out there."

"If I hadn't kept that key, I probably *would* have died." She wrapped her arms around her stomach, the chill of that fearful walk washing over her. "Once I got back to the room, I must have slept for an hour or two. Then I woke, unable to remember anything."

Her every fear had been worse than she'd imagined. She'd been right to question her judgment. She'd trusted and loved a man capable of unspeakable things.

And he had Evan.

How could she even think about baring her heart to anyone again? At the moment, she couldn't think of anything other than finding her son.

The front door opened. A shaft of frigid air blasted over her as it had that first day she'd woken here. Two uniformed officers stomped snow off their boots. Dee recognized one of them from the day she'd filed her report in Tacoma.

Again, she would have to tell her story, only this time it would be public knowledge. She straightened her spine and squeezed her hands together until they tingled.

Drained to her toes, she didn't relish baring to the world what a mess she'd made of her life. However, maternal instincts fired her beyond normal endurance. She looked at Jacob and gave a fleeting thought to leaning on him while she talked, but tossed the notion aside. Jacob didn't need the burden of her troubles, problems even worse than she could have imagined. She would do this the best way for both of them…alone.

"I need to report a kidnapping."

Two hours later, Jacob watched the cop slam the police cruiser door shut with Chase inside.

The noise jarred all the way through him. The officer planned to scare the spit out of Chase for his own good. Knowing this was the right thing didn't stop him from wanting to grab Chase by the scruff of the neck and send him home like a kid who'd been caught snitching cookies.

Two hundred and twenty dollars' worth of cookies, not to mention frightening the hell out of Dee tonight. And what about the lipstick incident on her bathroom mirror? Could that have been Chase, too? But why would he do that to Dee? *Deirdre.*

His jaw clenched even as he thought of her bastard of an ex-husband. Jacob forced himself to relax. He would deal with all of those feelings later. First, he had to settle Emily.

She slouched outside the door to her suite, the baby monitor clutched in her hand. He didn't need to step any closer. Even in the dimly lit parking lot he could see well enough the accusation in her eyes, along with unshed tears. She didn't understand why he'd turned in Chase.

How many more times would Chase let Emily down before she realized she deserved better? But then even Dee, an adult, had been blinded by love. Love for another man.

God, he felt hollowed out inside. He just wanted to give his kid sister a hug she no doubt needed.

Jacob stepped forward, but Emily backed away, into her room, closing the door quietly—but firmly. Maybe she would be calmer, more reasonable, in the morning.

Yeah, right. Jacob shrugged through half the kinks in his shoulders and climbed the porch steps toward Dee, slower than when he'd charged up them earlier.

As much as he'd lost, she'd lost more. He sliced away his own needs, safer for him, anyway, and focused on hers.

Jacob pushed through the motel door and found her curled in the corner of the sofa staring out the window. He tossed his coat onto the coat tree.

Dee gnawed on a fingernail. "I should have gone with the cops."

"You know there's nothing you can do at the police station tonight. They have the number here. Maybe they'll have some answers when we head into town tomorrow."

Dee dangled her arm along the couch back, her fingers drawing little circles in the condensation on the window. Outside, snow began spiraling from the sky, heralding an approaching storm. "Blane could be anywhere by now."

He knew that, but she didn't need it confirmed. "The authorities were searching blind before. Not now."

Dee exploded from the sofa. "I can't just sit here and do nothing. I have to find them."

"You need to be patient a little while longer."

She ripped a coat off the rack. A surplus of adrenaline oozed from her. "My son's out there somewhere. He's only four. He can't sleep without his airplane blanket and a story before bed. He's never been separated from me for more than three nights at Blane's, and Evan has a life-threatening peanut allergy. I can't just wait here and do nothing. I never should have let that cop persuade me to sit tight."

He shouldn't have been surprised by her frenzy. She'd held it together throughout a hellish night. From past experiences in combat, he'd seen enough to know the adrenaline letdown would crash into her soon.

Two long strides and he caught her. He grabbed her arm just as she reached for the door. "You've done everything you can. Filing a police report. Calling everyone you could think of who might have had contact with your ex-husband."

"It's not enough." She tried to wrench her wrist free, then flailed with her other. Her pitch rose, approaching hysteria. She jerked, scratched, kicked with surprising strength. "Jacob, damn it, let me go. I have to do something."

He trapped both of her wrists and gave her a light shake. "Think. Even if I gave you the keys to the truck and a full tank of gas, what more can you do tonight?"

Reason returned to her eyes just before they flooded with tears. She sagged like a rag doll in his grip. "There really isn't anything I can do, is there?"

"No, Dee, I'm afraid there isn't."

She crumpled against his chest. "Oh God, Jacob, this is so much worse than not knowing. I didn't think anything could hurt that much, but I was so wrong."

"I know." Jacob gentled his hands along her hair again. He gritted his teeth against the need to bury his face in her neck. "I know."

"Hold me. Please." Half sobbing, gasping in air, she burrowed against his chest.

She squirmed against him as if to nestle closer still. He tried to ignore his reaction to her soft body wriggling against his. As much as he wanted, needed, burned to lose himself inside her and forget about the whole damned evening, she needed something else from him.

Or so he thought.

Her hands grappled at his shirt, his shoulders, his hair, dragging his head down to hers. Tapping the last dregs of his self-control, he held himself back.

With a none-too-gentle yank, Dee urged him closer. "Kiss me, damn it."

He wanted to, needed to, but knew it was wrong. The wrong time. The wrong reason. But she sure as hell felt like the right woman. "You don't know what you're saying. It's adrenaline talking."

Fire snapped from her eyes, full force and full of will. "Adrenaline? Is that what it was yesterday? Or every day we've been together and I wanted this?" Her pupils widened until her eyes turned near-black, like heavy storm clouds. "For all this time I've been trying to remember, yet now I'm finding I desperately need to forget. Please, for just a few hours, help me forget."

Good intentions fled. All his honorable platitudes seemed to have checked out for the night, and he couldn't think of a single rebuttal. His fingers flexed around her wrists as he stared into the tear-misted eyes of this woman he wanted more than air.

Time to quit fighting it. He hadn't been able to walk away from her the first time he saw her any more than he could turn away now.

Chapter 12

Was she getting through to him? If he turned her down, she would—

Do what?

Shriek her frustration at him and the whole world? She'd already done enough shouting for one night, for a lifetime even.

But the very trait that made Jacob so attractive to her could be the one thing that caused him to pull away. The man was so honorable.

She needed to forget what Blane had done to her and their child. Just for tonight until she could do something to find Evan.

"Jacob," she moaned, demanded. Determination

fueled her fingers as she shoved his buttons free, working her way from his neck down the camouflage uniform. All those necessary layers of cold-weather wear kept her from finding the salty skin she yearned to taste. She groaned her frustration. His hands covered hers.

Uh-oh. Here comes more talk of right and wrong and morning-after regrets.

Stretching onto her toes, Dee grazed her mouth along his neck, up to his ear. She'd never considered herself much of a femme fatale and feared she would fall short now. Blane's infidelity had torn at her self-confidence. He'd been her first, and after their split, she'd shut that part of her away rather than risk more rejection.

Would she have ever pursued Jacob so relentlessly before she'd lost her memory? Of course not. How odd that it had taken a hefty dose of amnesia to set her sensuality free. Still, she wasn't sure her fledgling sense of adventure could withstand Jacob turning from her.

Pride forced a huskiness to her voice. "Don't tell me 'no.'"

"All right."

That stopped her faster than any long speech about impulsive mistakes. Pride ducked behind surprise.

Dee's grip tightened around Jacob's collar. "You don't think this is a bad idea? You don't think it's an adrenaline high that—"

Jacob silenced her with a hard kiss.

He rested his forehead against hers. "Yes, I do

think we're both riding an adrenaline high. But no, I don't think we should stop. We've both wanted this too long to waste it by rushing. Let's take it slow." His light blue eyes turned smoky, whispering over her. "Really slow."

The hungry sweep of his eyes left Dee with no doubts. He wasn't going to leave her hurting and alone. Relief turned her legs to soup, like one of those Sunday Jell-O molds left out too long.

It was going to happen. She and Jacob would be naked in a matter of moments—slow, stolen moments.

He dipped his head to drink unending, leisurely kisses from her mouth. What made the feel of his hands on her so special, so different?

She met his questing tongue with her own, reacquainting herself with the mind-numbing taste of Jacob. Liquid fire poured straight through her like a swig of his beer.

He looped an arm around her waist to mesh their bodies and walked her with him, their synchronized steps almost dancelike. Jacob locked the door, flicked a switch activating the No Vacancy light in the window, and backed her into his apartment, never once halting his deliberate homage to her lips. Every brush of their bodies against each other nudged his solid arousal against her stomach, a reminder, a promise.

Jacob backed her across his darkened apartment until they stood bathed in the moonbeams streaming through the skylight. True to his word, he peeled away her clothes with torturous precision. His broad hands tunneled beneath the sweatshirt as inch by shivery inch, he bunched the fabric up and free.

Her yellow floral shirt hung loose, draping over her breasts. Jacob fingered the small rips where there had once been pearly buttons. His jaw flexed, and she feared the mood had been broken.

"Jacob?"

Groaning, he pressed her to him. "I should have been here for you."

She feathered her fingers over his brows. So many shadows lingered in his eyes. Insecurities nipped. What did she have to offer? Very little according to Blane.

She could give Jacob reassurance. "You've been there for me since the second I first walked into the lobby. You're here now."

"Not a real hardship tour, being here for you tonight."

In spite of his lighthearted tone, Dee searched his eyes and found a mirror of her own thoughts, an appreciation for the rare window of time they had together.

She cupped his face in her hands. "I need you. I need you so much tonight."

Suddenly slow didn't seem as important as the urge to be closer. She reached for him as he reached for her. Their hands dodged each other to stroke aside clothes and any lingering inhibitions. They made their way up the loft steps, leaving a path behind them.

Camouflage draped over yellow flowered flannel.

Rugged thermal rested beneath a white lace bra.

When they reached the top step, she wore nothing but her panties. He wore nothing at all.

Moonlight caressed every inch of Jacob as she longed to. She walked her fingers down his chest, her skin so pale against the bronzed vitality of him. So much strength beneath her hands and she ached to soak some of it up to carry her through the coming days.

He grazed the backs of his fingers along her jaw, her neck, between her breasts. She gasped, her mouth drying as moist heat pooled between her legs.

Jacob sealed his mouth to hers, probing deeply, fully, as he would later do with his body. Her senses already heightened from an evening of too much emotion, she hooked her arms around his neck and simply hung on.

His hands roved, possessed, until he splayed one hand along the middle of her back, the other cupping her bottom. He lifted her, trailing kisses along her jaw. Raised her higher still, his mouth nibbling down her neck.

Jacob kissed a moist path between her breasts. Her breath hitched in anticipation. He lingered until she wanted to yank his hair in frustration.

"Jacob, forget slow."

She felt his smile against her skin, another tantalizing brush that pulled the thread of desire tauter within her. He puffed a teasing blast of air over her just before he latched on. She exhaled, shuddered and arched in a silent invitation for more.

Dee braced her hands on his shoulders, her arms trembling as her legs dangled. He laved equal attention on her other breast, feasting alternately from both until her head fell back. Her hair swayed along her spine, sending a fresh tingle along her already-shimmering nerves.

Jacob lowered her to his bed, and in the flash of time before he joined her, Dee devoured him with her gaze. The very size of him thrilled her. Six foot four inches of muscled man, all hard and eager for *her*.

Then he hooked his thumbs in her panties, and she froze. How could she have forgotten? Her scar would glare, bringing the world rushing back between them. Already tears stung. A band of pain constricted her ribs.

He hovered over her, his brows knit together, his breathing rasping as if he'd shoveled the whole parking lot. "Do you want to stop?"

Definitely not. "No."

His exhaled enough relief to combat the best Washington storm wind. "What's wrong, then? What do you need?"

"Nothing. Just don't stop, please."

His eyes never left her face as he skimmed her panties down her legs and to the floor. Instinctively her hand flew to her stomach and covered the place where her baby had once rested, where a scar remained.

Jacob's gaze snapped to her protective hand. His brow smoothed before he circled her wrist and eased her arm away. With one thumb, he soothed the faded incision before he placed his broad palm on her belly. His fingers splayed over her stomach with healing heat. "We'll find him."

Determination rang from his vow. She wanted to believe him. Even if placing so much trust in him screamed of losing control, she wasn't left with any choice. If ever a man could accomplish something through sheer will, she believed Jacob could.

Her hand fluttered to rest over his, linking. Then he joined her on the bed. Dee scooched up the quilt as he shadowed her body with his, finally blanketing her without letting go of her hand.

She gripped his fingers tighter and held on. That connection, something so basic and beyond the sexual, anchored her. Just as his friendship had moored her through a time when she could very well have drifted into dangerous waters. She squeezed his hand. "Make me forget. Make us both forget."

"I'll damn well try my best." His callused hands snagged along her skin with a sweet abrasion.

Dee lost herself in a swirl of sensations, his warm body beneath her fingers. She smoothed over his chest, traced a ridged scar along his arm. She shivered at how close he'd come to dying that day.

His strong, columned neck smelled of wind and musk. She sketched along the muscles on his chest, his abs, lower. As her hand curled around his rigid length, exploring, learning him, she found his need obviously equaled hers.

Jacob skimmed her scar once again, but continued lower until he cradled the core of her. He circled and soothed until she writhed against him. A lone finger dipped and dampened to rub the sensitive bundle of nerves.

So much, almost too much, the intensity built. But she knew where it would lead, or rather wouldn't, and she didn't want their time ruined by his disappointment.

She clasped his wrist, tugging his hand upward again.

Jacob nuzzled her neck and tugged back. "Not yet. Not until you've—"

"It's okay." She rocked her hips, seeking to distract him. A hint of desperation leaked into her voice. "We have all night."

He pulled back and braced on both forearms. "What's going on?"

"Nothing. I'm just ready." Shards of inadequacy pelted her, and she tried desperately to dodge them. She didn't want Blane's insults to have power over her ever again, especially not now.

"Like you said, we have all night."

His hand soothed her again, sending tantalizing yet frustrating ripples through her. She couldn't bear to see his disappointment, so she turned her face away before she spoke. "Jacob. I can't. Okay? I don't, uh, finish."

The stroking stopped, and she wasn't sure whether to be grateful or not.

"You've never had an—"

"Jacob—" She clapped her hand over his mouth. Heat crept up her face. Why couldn't she have been more tempting, more *anything* to have lured him past this point before he found out? "I guess that's something else I forgot when I was throwing myself at you. It doesn't have to make a difference now." She teased her fingertips along his back, over his buttocks and up again. "Being close to you, that's what I want, what I need. It's enough for me, really."

During her whole rambling speech, he stared at her with those piercing eyes that saw straight to a person's soul without allowing a reciprocal peek. "Let me ask you something."

Why did they have to talk? "What?"

"Does this feel good?" The backs of his fingers flicked over her breast. "And this?" He reached lower. "Does it?"

"Yes," she gasped, "but—"

"Then why rush?" He kissed her protest away. "You say it won't finish the way I think it will. So? If you're enjoying it, don't push me away just because of what you think I expect."

It made sense. If only she could believe he meant it. Knowing Jacob, he probably thought he could succeed where eight years in a marriage bed hadn't. She cringed, envisioning the realization that would steal over his face as minutes passed and he accepted that he'd failed. She'd failed.

He breathed against her lips. "Trust me."

She wanted to do just that and simply bask in the warm tension building from his persistent touch. Where Deirdre would insist he stop, Dee would have taken a risk and let him continue.

How very much she wanted Dee's boldness. She could have it, for tonight with Jacob. Dee was the woman he knew, the woman he'd taken to bed.

She closed her eyes, forgot about passing minutes or possible goals and savored. She gathered every sensation like a treasured gift, the glide of fingers, the caress of lips along her ear as he whispered all the ways he longed to love her body.

Release crashed over her without warning. Like a wave slapping her, almost painful in its intensity, leaving her struggling for air. Her back bowed off the bed, driving his hand harder, his finger deeper and sending a fresh wave pulsing through her, building until her cries of pleasure rode on the last rush.

Reality returned in increments. The stars faintly visible through the swirl of snow along the skylight. Jacob sweeping her hair away from her face. His leg nestled between her thighs, a heavy, delicious burden.

Dee loosened her fingernail-deep grip on his hip, and his mouth tipped in a hint of a smile. His eyes cleared, and he let her in for a rare look that said far more than words. Her friend had returned. Only a hint of male pride gleamed in his eyes, mingling with happiness for her.

When her heart had slowed to something resembling a slow jog, she squeezed his hand. He dropped a kiss to her forehead and rolled away. Dee almost shouted her frustration until she saw him delve into his bedside table and pull out a small, square cellophane packet.

A totally irrational wad of jealousy punched her. She chewed the insides of her mouth to keep from asking him whom he'd bought them for.

Jacob glanced at her. "After that night in the back of my truck."

"What?"

"I bought a box the next day. I told myself we shouldn't end up here. Having these around still seemed smart."

"Very smart."

He sheathed himself and tucked her beneath him again. With the quilt under her, Jacob over her and the stars glimmering through the skylight above, Dee couldn't help but remember that kiss. How much he'd needed her then. How much they needed each other now.

Eyes locked on each other, he entered her slowly, as her body stretched to accommodate him. He stilled, bearing the bulk of his weight on his forearms. She gazed up at him, almost seeing him anew during that instant of being joined for the first time.

Then he moved, and she lost the ability to think about beginnings—inevitable endings. So long. It had been so long, if ever, since she'd felt such an incredible heightened sense of awareness. Rather than forgetfulness, she'd found an awakening that surpassed anything she could have wished for.

They found the rhythm unique to their union, neared the edge and fought it off, prolonging the sensations like a gift that would be snatched away once they accepted it.

Finally his heaving chest, their sweat-slicked bodies,

signaled an end, and she almost mourned the pleasure she knew was an instant away. Again, his hand found her, circled, a single nudge sending her spiraling until she felt as if she'd flown through the skylight, free-falling into the night.

With a hoarse shout, he joined her. She reached to hold his hand as her body accepted him.

She feared her heart wasn't far behind.

With Dee's sleeping body curled against him, Jacob could almost allow himself to forget they had to put their feet on the floor and resume life in a few hours.

Gently he loosened her grip on his hand. When she didn't stir, he draped the quilt over her arm and up to her creamy, bare shoulders. He skimmed his thumb along her collarbone, to the hollow of her throat.

Already he stirred again at even the thought of crawling beneath that quilt and losing himself inside her. If he thought once more would satisfy his need for her, he would. But he knew it wouldn't be enough.

Jacob snatched his hand away and shoved to his feet.

It was only supposed to be about sex, a release, a momentary escape for both of them. Of course, it could have been all about sex for her. How clearly he could see her beautiful face flooding with surprise just before shifting to lazy-lidded pleasure.

He bit off a curse. The last thing he wanted from her was gratitude for introducing her to good sex. *Great* sex.

His need for more told him he'd already gotten too

close. She'd become too important. He should back up, gain distance and perspective for her sake as well as his.

Jacob whipped a pair of sweatpants off the back of a chair and slid into them. Each step from the loft should have offered him the distance he needed. Instead her every breath whispered through the room, tempting him. Even the skylight seemed to silhouette her in some center-stage way.

Where did they go from here tomorrow?

Thinking of Chase in lock-up for the night, Jacob scrubbed a hand over the back of his neck. His hormones had been so tied in knots over Dee, he'd let his guard down and messed up with Chase. His hormones could cost him focus in finding her child.

Still, he couldn't turn his back on her now. Jacob dropped into the recliner and tapped the telephone beside him.

He wasn't sure he could be the kind of man she wanted long-term, but he could sure as hell help her with her here and now. No more waiting to get back on the job. With sunrise nearing, it was time to tap into the extra help his military network could provide.

Chapter 13

Sitting on the edge of the bed, Dee faced the morning with a mix of anticipation and dread. She clutched the telephone after speaking with her parents in Colorado about taking a photo to their local police station. She wanted to believe she would be holding her child just as tightly by the end of the day.

Through the skylight the clouds hovered above, heavy and gray as the first morning light fought the overcast conditions as fiercely as she struggled to keep her mood positive, to hold on to the comfort she'd found in Jacob's embrace through the night.

He paced in the hall, cell phone to his ear. He moved with tense, purposeful strides, freshly showered and wearing his flight suit for a trip to the base after they spoke with the police. He'd already been on his cell when she woke up, still talking when she took her shower and then called her parents. She itched to know what he'd uncovered.

Replacing the cordless receiver into the charger, she listened to Jacob's end of his cell phone conversation.

"They've updated the APB on Lambert, including the boy?... Good... Uh-huh... Even better."

Hope surged through her. She tugged her pink sweater over the low waistband of her jeans, the cashmere a poor substitute for Jacob's embrace, and padded down the loft steps.

"Any hits from the ferries at Puget Sound?" His gaze flicked over to her, lingered for a moment, smoked with a banked fire, then his attention returned to the conversation. "Uh-huh. I'll see if she can come up with anything more about his plans to cross the border."

Could he have already found a lead? Her emotions as tender as her body, she craved even a sliver of reassurance that her son would be in her arms soon. Jacob certainly appeared invincible, capable of anything in his flight suit.

Even in socks and no boots.

"Yeah. Thanks for getting back to me so quickly, Spike. Tell your Mountie bud I owe him." He thumbed the off button on the cell and looked at Dee.

"Well?" She could see her answer in his eyes, and it wasn't good. She'd told herself not to hope, but that didn't stop the stab of disappointment.

"I've been talking to a friend on base with the Office of Special Investigation to see if they could get any inside scoop since your ex was up on charges that would affect military safety."

"The man you called Spike?"

"Right, Special Agent Keagan. We've been back and forth on the phone for a few hours now."

"And he said?" She scrambled to process all he was telling her, but kept thinking of how her husband had put all of these military people in danger just for money. She hoped all the potential damage had come to light when his partner had been arrested, but could there be more?

Finding Blane became even more important, something she wouldn't have thought possible.

"The cops have updated the data in the NCIC— National Crime Information Center. A warrant had already been issued for Lambert's arrest for custodial interference based on your statement to the police last night. They've put a trace on all his credit cards and his cell phone. They're also keeping an eye on his, uh, mistress. Her phone records will be monitored, as well. I wish I had more for you."

"You've done so much. Thank you." She hadn't thought about him taking the other woman along later. At least the policeman last night had the forethought to jot down the woman's name. Then the rest of Jacob's words trickled through her brain. "You said you've been speaking with him off and on for hours. Did you manage to snatch any sleep?"

His gaze flicked to the bed, with its rumpled sheets and musky air of sex. "I'm used to catching power-naps when we have a long flight." He cocked his head to the side. "How did the conversation with your parents go?"

"Simple. Everything's taken care of on their end."

"That rough, huh?" He stepped closer, a simple reach away, the uniform stretching across the broad chest she'd slept against through the night.

She tried not to let the hollowness inside her echo through to her voice. "They're not demonstrative people, and we haven't spoken in so long. I didn't expect a great emotional outpouring. They'll take care of what needs doing with Evan's picture. Wiring me money. That's all I can ask."

Indignation snapped in his eyes. "I happen to think you can ask for about anything you need at a time like this. For what it's worth, I'm here for you, and that includes helping you through this."

For all of four more days remaining in his leave time?

The words went unspoken between them. Still she could almost hear the clock ticking away their time together. She wanted to believe she would be holding Evan by nightfall, but she had to accept the reality that she could be searching for him for a long while—on her own.

An uncomfortable silence stretched. Morning-after awkwardness? Maybe. She hadn't expected declarations of undying love, certainly wasn't sure she could have handled it if he'd said any such thing. Her one brush with love and marriage had left her burned beyond belief.

All past problems aside, because of Evan she couldn't think beyond the next few hours, much less into any kind of future. She needed to hold on to the hope that with her returned memory, she would find her son. "I'll scrounge up some breakfast."

Jacob watched Dee make tracks toward the door, her signature spunk starching all the way up her spine. He hated that his rotten mood had kept him from reaching out to her after sex.

The phone calls—his and hers—had left him frustrated, edgy and feeling too damned inadequate. She deserved better from him.

Halfway across the room, she paused. "What?"

"We don't have to leave for another hour. There's nothing to accomplish by showing up early." He extended his arms. "Come here."

Still she hesitated.

Dee usually had such a grab-life attitude, he kept forgetting about those tender feelings. He could use the time to gather more information about her past while indulging her in some morning-after cuddling women seemed to need. "We've watched a lot of sunsets together." He nodded to the picture window across the room. "Let's watch a sunrise."

At the mention of their ritual after supper, her shoulders relaxed. She inched toward him.

He spread his arms wider. "Come here."

"Come get me."

Jacob couldn't hold back the smile. His Dee had returned, and he'd missed her even during those few short minutes she'd been gone.

He tugged her arm as he sank into the recliner. She curved into him as he settled his chin on her head. A perfect fit. "My ID of the man who checked you in matches Lambert's description. The search was broad before, but now they're checking out ferries, bus stations, airlines. The border patrol has been alerted."

"Two weeks too late. He's probably already left the country."

"So they'll find him in Canada."

Her bare foot peeked from the hem of her jeans. He smiled, remembering her surprise that first day at finding she had big feet. Jacob cupped the graceful arch in his hand and warmed her skin. "That picture from your parents will be a big help to the police."

Dee stiffened in his arms, hesitated, then said, "Their photo will be at least six months old. Hopefully somebody can get to one of my more recent snapshots soon."

Six months old? Odd. His friends all had pictures of their kids littering tabletops and albums, a new batch cropping up almost by the week. "It's better than nothing until somebody gets to yours."

She shifted in his lap, her bottom wiggling against him again. Jacob gritted his teeth, damn near cracked a crown.

Her face rested against his chest, her lashes fluttering

against his skin. He tamped down temptation, then shot it all to hell by tunneling his hand under the quilt to cup her warm skin. She sighed and sagged into his touch.

Patting her back wasn't enough. He needed to fix her whole world and make sure no one ever hurt her again. "It's going to be all right."

Dee swiped her wrist under her nose. "I hope so. It's just tough to trust my judgment after the way I fell for a man like that. I haven't spoken to my parents in years. Other than sending them an occasional picture of Evan, we haven't had contact since I married Blane."

That explained the old picture. But it didn't explain how a parent gave up on a child. That he couldn't understand. Hadn't anyone stood by this woman the way she deserved? "How long were you married?"

"Eight years."

"You married young, then." And went right from her unforgiving parents to an unfaithful husband. No wonder she instinctively resisted leaning on anyone.

"I was a late-in-life child for my parents. They petted me, took care of everything for me. Sounds pretty pathetic when I say it out loud." She traced along a patch on his sleeve, her fingers sketching over a stitched flag. "They didn't like Blane. I made my first big stand in marrying him, and was too prideful to admit to them I was wrong."

"Everybody makes mistakes. That's life. Sounds like your parents didn't give you a chance to learn from making them."

Dee's hand abandoned the quilt to cup his face.

"You're sweet, trying to let me off the hook like that, but I'm responsible, too. I can't bear to think of all the military members he has put in jeopardy for greed."

He couldn't let himself think overlong on how the man had been sending defective parts for the very planes Jacob had worked to keep in perfect condition. A crash because of mechanical failure would be a guilt he couldn't live with.

His grip tightened and Dee winced. He stared into those brown eyes and saw the hurt and shame she couldn't hide. "Dee, it's not your fault. None of it. You're not responsible for what your husband did and you're not to blame for how your parents have acted."

He kissed her before she could argue, because he couldn't wait another minute to taste her, and because he knew she'd have to close her eyes.

Dee ended the kiss with a brief tug on his bottom lip. "Guess I inherited that stiff-necked prideful nature from my parents, a part of why they had no reason to miss us when Blane dumped me in the middle of nowhere."

What would happen to Emily and Madison if the next time he flew into combat, he didn't make it home? Chase hadn't proven himself to be much in the way of support—emotional or otherwise. Jacob's grip around Dee tightened. He couldn't stand to think of his sister as vulnerable and alone as this woman.

She snuggled closer and continued talking. "It still gives me chills to think of how easily I fell off the map.

I'd quit my job to move away from Blane, so even my friends weren't expecting to hear anything from me. I'd put all my furniture in storage and moved into a resort weekly rental condo while I lined up job interviews in nearby towns midyear—I'm a preschool teacher."

"That explains your obsession with hats." And why she'd been so good with Emily and Madison.

Jacob's arms twitched protectively around Dee as his thoughts flew back to the previous night. Chase would spend another few hours in jail before his parents would be able to spring him. Jacob forced his breathing to level out and reminded himself he hadn't had a choice.

No one would hurt her again, not Chase, not her worthless son of a bitch ex-husband.

Jacob thought of the uncharacteristic red dress. Another clue he'd missed. His instincts had all but clubbed him over the head that the clothes didn't match the woman inside. "The red dress wasn't yours?"

She shuddered. "Not even close."

"Lambert?"

"He tossed out my clothes when I was sleeping. I still can't believe I even managed to fall asleep that night. I just remember lying down beside Evan to help him settle and I must have drifted off for a few minutes out of sheer exhaustion. When I woke, he'd undressed me, thrown out my clothes and had that red dress waiting. Just the style his mistress liked." Shuddering, Dee tugged the blanket closer around herself. "Blane always did have a sick sense of humor. I could have died out there without warm clothes and he would have gotten away with Evan."

Jacob's muscles contracted, and he forced himself not to hold her too tightly. He wanted to kill Lambert, with his hands, a gun, it didn't matter.

Dee squirmed in his arms, and Jacob loosened his hold. "Sorry."

"It's okay." She snuggled closer as rays of sunshine pushed through the clouds to glitter off the picture window glass.

Their night together had ended.

Dee stared at the computer screen in the police cubicle. Her picture stared right back from a god-awful driver's license photo. Shoulder-length hair had been restrained with a headband. Her smile was overbright, her eyes wide as if the flash had caught her unawares.

Little had she known how life would blindside her just as unexpectedly.

Amazing how much younger she'd looked a mere three years ago, mistakenly thinking she had her world in order—marriage, son, job. All a sham. A false sense of security. She'd been too young and trusting. Not anymore. She owed Evan.

She also owed Jacob for his faith when he'd had no reason to take her in. Steady and constant, he sat next to her, walking her through the process of telling her story—again.

The detective nodded to the computer. "Okay now, Mrs. Lambert. You're who you say you are."

Startled, Dee glanced up. "Of course I am."

"Well, ma'am." The older man scratched a hand along his graying buzz cut. "No disrespect meant, but it wasn't a given without some kind of confirmation. We have a saying around here. 'In God we trust—'"

"'But everyone else is suspect,'" Jacob finished.

Dee glanced from one to the other, both so confident, both with hundred-year-old cynical eyes. She needed to be more like them to survive. "What a way to live."

The detective clicked the keys and a new image emerged. "Your husband, ma'am?"

Unable to scrounge enough spit to speak, Dee stared at the photo of Blane, blond, wiry and too handsome for words even in a mug shot.

The corner of Jacob's eye twitched. "Her ex-husband?"

She nodded. Part of her wanted to tell them all this wasn't happening, deny she'd even met that traitorous toad. She would simply ditch her Deirdre Lambert self. Except she'd already learned the past couldn't simply be ignored. The past had happened, as she remembered clearly now. Her child's father would have a criminal record.

What a heritage for her son to carry.

She grieved for Evan that she hadn't chosen more wisely. Yet without Blane, she wouldn't have Evan.

The chair creaked as the cop leaned back. "We're monitoring his accounts, tracking for any credit card activity, keeping a watch on his cell phone account and his girlfriend's telephone. If he's found over the border, a Canadian arrest warrant will have to be issued, along with a request for extradition."

Jacob nodded through the steps, but Dee's head was reeling. "Even if we find Blane, I'll have to wait for a bunch of diplomatic mumbo jumbo to clear before they can arrest him."

"Ma'am, I know it sounds—"

"It sounds like he'll have enough warning to run with my son again—" She forced her breathing to even out. "Sorry. I just want him back."

"Of course you do." The older officer clicked through a series of codes and the screen changed again. "This came through just before you arrived."

A child's face appeared. Evan's face. She bit back a cry.

Jacob braced a hand low on her back. "Other than the hair color, he looks just like you."

She nodded, unable to speak without letting loose a flood of tears.

The detective pivoted back to the screen, the chair squeaking a low keen. "He will be logged into the data base for the NCMEC—National Center for Missing and Exploited Children."

She twisted her hands together, but they still shook. Her child was on his way to appearing on a milk carton.

Her hand gravitated toward the computer screen as

if she could somehow touch Evan. The silky blond hair. The gap between his front teeth that showed when he smiled, which he did often. Her shy but happy child.

"He's so little, only three—" She pressed the back of her wrist to her mouth. "No wait. He had his fourth birthday a week ago, and I missed it." Anger kicked through her, steeling her spine. "Damn Blane for taking that away from me, too—"

She stopped short as two police officers with snow on their shoulders approached the cubicle, both with sober expressions.

Anxiety gripped her stomach. The cops both looked at Jacob, who promptly slid a bracing arm around her shoulders.

Her spine stiffened. "Don't try to break the news gently. I want to know what's going on."

The older of the two policemen stepped closer, his expression shifting to one of total sympathy. "Ma'am, we checked the highway location you gave the officer last night and we found the spot where you struggled with your husband. The road was clear enough for us to see tread marks. So we blocked off the lane and swept away the rest of the snow."

Tread marks? What was the worry over some leftover rubber? She stifled hysterical laughter. "He sped away. Of course he skidded for a moment."

"Ma'am, the tread marks lead into the river."

Jacob's arm tightened around her even as he remained silent.

She blinked fast, unable to process what she was hearing. "I saw him leave. I saw it."

The policeman fidgeted with his hat in his hands. "They've already uncovered the vehicle—" he paused, then gentled his voice further "—and a man's body."

She shook her head, gasping gulps of air. Pain blinded her, stabbed through her whole body into a great gaping hole in her heart. "No. No, no, no, I saw them drive away. My memory is clear now."

Nausea swamped her at even the possibility they suggested. But it couldn't be true.

It. Was. Not. True.

My God, hadn't she seen the Suburban leave?

The detective behind the desk rolled his chair closer, his elbows on his knees. "You need to prepare yourself and consider that you could be remembering what you wanted to see. You suffered a head injury. Your brain could still be trying to protect you from what you saw."

No. The mind couldn't be so deceitful. Still, uncertainty nipped her.

If the officers were right, that meant her child was…dead. An unbearable thought.

Unbearable enough to make her lose her mind completely after all?

Chapter 14

He hated being confined this way, in a tiny room with nothing much more than a too-small bed and a couple of dreary windows. But he had to keep a low profile now more than ever.

At least he could be grateful the police hadn't uncovered anything more about him. Beyond the incident with Dee, which could be easily explained away, they had nothing on him. He intended to keep it that way so he could start his new life, free of past mistakes.

He just had to figure out what to do about the kid, then he could move forward. He shifted on the crummy mattress, dreaming of the day when he would have a new place of his own with first-class bedsprings and a big-ass television. Not much longer and he would have everything he required—the money—to make his move. He simply needed to be patient.

If only patience didn't involve confinement to a lone room when he wanted to be outside, on the move. Free.

And it was all Dee's fault, damn her.

Yeah, he wanted a clean break. But he also craved revenge.

He wondered which urge would win.

The biting wind slapped Dee's face as she walked with Jacob down the cement steps, stirring smaller memories of her son, how he needed his ears covered. Evan succumbed to infections so easily.

What a ridiculous thought when he really could be dead. The full import of the possibility hadn't hit her. This wasn't denial, damn it, because she refused to believe it was true in the first place.

She simply followed Jacob, numb, climbing into his truck. A few miles later—how many she wasn't sure— she blinked through her fog enough to look around and realize… "Jacob, you turned the wrong way."

His eyes stayed forward with unwavering focus. "No, I didn't."

"Where are we going?"

"To base."

"Base? I know you'd planned that originally, but things have—" she swallowed hard "—things have changed given what the police found in the river."

Maybe he was taking her to the military doctor again. Perhaps he thought she'd totally lost it.

His hands stayed steady on the steering wheel as the truck charged ahead. "You told me you saw your ex drive off with your son."

"But the skid marks…"

"There must be some other explanation," he said with unshakable conviction.

Hope teased at her insides. "How can you be sure?"

He glanced in her direction, his strong jaw as set as his voice. "I heard it in your voice. You know what you saw."

He believed her, even when she could barely believe in herself. The notion rocked her hard at a time when she already wasn't feeling too steady. But if Jacob thought there was a chance Evan wasn't in that river, she would grasp on to that possibility with both hands.

She wouldn't give up on her child as long as there was any chance to find him. "Your friend Spike?"

"If I ask him to keep looking for information on your ex, he will search."

Hope fanned stronger, hotter, burning away the fog of grief clouding her mind. "They're even coming in on a weekend."

"They're already waiting. It's not that I don't trust the police. I just believe the more people we have working on this, the better." He passed her his cell phone. "While we're driving, you should check your voice mail on the phone at your new place and on your cell."

She should have thought of that herself. Thank

goodness Jacob covered all possibilities, even if this was a long shot. The police hadn't tracked any calls from Blane's cell. Still, she might find something else and right now any tiny lead felt vital to her sanity and to her son's safety.

Phone gripped in her hand, she started punching in the access code she now remembered. How wonderful to have such a basic part of her life back.

And most wonderful of all, Jacob believed her.

He hadn't given up. He'd navigated the necessary official channels, and now they would strike out on their own. After so long of depending only on herself, this felt surreal. Wonderful. Almost too much.

Too easily she could grow accustomed to this sort of support, then how would she survive on her own again?

Jacob walked with security through the multiple doors closing off the OSI offices from even the protected confines of a military base. If there were answers to be found, he trusted they would surface here.

He would have liked to come here first, but recognized the need to go through official steps beforehand. The police needed as much information as possible. And the time he and Dee had spent speaking with them gave his friends a chance to follow up on their own leads.

Dee's calls to check her messages hadn't netted anything but a few telemarketing hang ups and two job offers. Pretty much what he'd expected. But he'd thought giving her something to do would help her feel more in control.

The last door hissed open as the vault door seal released. Inside waited Special Agent Max Keagan, along with a couple of crew friends—Bronco and Crusty. The two pilots, both family men, appeared solemn faced. No doubt envisioning the hell of this happening to one of their children. Jacob hadn't spent much time with Madison, but the little angel had a way of wrapping her fingers tightly around a person's heart.

He could only imagine what Dee was going through.

Dee looked around. "I don't even know how to say thank you. You've all gone above and beyond."

Bronco lumbered up from his chair and offered it to her. "This is what we do for each other. If you're with Jacob, that makes you one of ours, remember? We take care of our own."

Special Agent Keagan scrubbed a hand over his spiked blond hair as he clicked through computer keys. He held up a hand in greeting but stayed silent.

Crusty produced a box of doughnuts. "He's been tapping into some connections at border patrol."

"In case they went to Canada." She shook her head as a no-thank-you to the food.

Crusty scooped up a jelly-filled pastry. "Right. There's camera footage at those stations and satellite photos. We're still looking into the possibility he hopped a ferry." He downed half the doughnut in one bite. "Spike's got all sorts of superspy tricks up his sleeve for narrowing the search."

Keagan's fingers slowed. Without turning away from his computer, he waved over his shoulder. "When was the lipstick-on-the-mirror incident? Exact date."

Jacob rattled off the information then asked, "Why? We thought that was Chase causing more trouble."

Keagan snagged a gulp from his bottled water before returning to the keyboard. "Maybe, maybe not. I'll check around and see if Lambert's crossing back and forth over the border. So far, though, there's not even a peep from him. He's not at work. No credit card activity."

Dee started shaking again. "They're not dead. They can't be."

Keagan patted the air in a calm-down motion. "I'm not saying they are. There are plenty of ways to pay for things without credit cards. Until I have definitive proof to the contrary, we're going to keep looking for your boy. My wife and I have a son, too." His gaze fell briefly to the photo of a newborn in blue grinning as he held a toy dolphin. "I'll search for your child as if he were my own."

Her hand shook as she reached to stroke a finger along the edge of the gold frame on the agent's desk. "Thank you."

Jacob hoped like hell that Dee was right about her ex driving off. "Would he really risk coming back here just to torment her? Why not make a clean run with Evan?"

"That would be the logical choice, but..." Keagan trailed off.

Dee's face turned paler. "He's not logical anymore.

Or rather, he's even more unbalanced than before, especially if he somehow found out I didn't die that night."

Jacob leaned forward, elbows braced on his knees. "Maybe he's buying time while he sets up a new identity. He wouldn't have had much warning that Dee was on to him."

Dee's eyes widened before blinking faster, darting from side to side. He couldn't imagine what it must be costing her to climb inside the mind of her crooked, cruel ex-husband.

Basically all the options here stunk.

Her ex and son could be dead. Or the criminal was on the road somewhere far away with her child.

Or Lambert was close by, determined to succeed in killing Dee this time.

Dee fidgeted with her seat belt as she watched Jacob charge up the steps back into the Lodge. He was closing the place—indefinitely. He planned to hide out with Dee in visitor's quarters on base, while sending Emily and Madison to stay with Grace and her family. Grace was already inside Emily's room helping her pack for the baby before they would leave together.

Meanwhile, Special Agent Keagan was still working his secret ops magic to pick up her ex-husband's trail.

She refused to consider the body in the river was Blane's. He'd simply ditched the vehicle. He was trying to cover his tracks.

And the dead body? She said a prayer for whoever had died, because she had to believe dental records would prove it wasn't Blane.

Everything was happening so fast. She'd known Jacob to be a man of action, yet his lightning-fast preparations left her head spinning. In his typical Jacob manner, he never seemed to hurry, yet arrangements had been made before she could blink.

Dee tucked her toes under the dash and soaked up the heater's blast, anything to keep her occupied. She'd already packed her meager gear earlier and brought it with her to the police station so she could be mobile if they found Evan. Now Jacob insisted she wait here for him while he finished a couple of last-minute details.

Damn, she was restless. After waiting so long, a few more hours shouldn't matter. But they did.

Her life had changed too much, too fast. She and Jacob had slept together, a new memory that needed to be analyzed, pondered, savored. Except fear for Evan left her nearly breathless.

As Jacob posted a Closed sign on the front entrance of the hotel, a room door swung wide. Emily stepped out, saw Jacob and stopped. He opened his mouth, and his sister shoved her hands deeper into her pockets. Emily's shoulders rose as her eyes turned sulky. Jacob's mouth closed. He nodded and turned away, disappearing inside.

Dee could hardly believe what she'd just seen. Emily couldn't actually be angry with Jacob. Chase had been the one in the wrong.

Except logic didn't always come into play with adolescent emotions.

Dee wanted to leap from the truck and shake Emily by her two layers of oversize sweaters. Instead Dee rolled down the window. The teacher in her wouldn't let the teen skulk away. "Emily? Over here."

Emily jerked and nearly slipped on a patch of ice, her heavy eye makeup smeared from tears. She glanced over her shoulder before turning back. Her feet skated along the ice as she warily approached.

The moody teen scratched her boot heel through the sludge, the baby monitor in hand as she hugged herself. "You doing okay?"

"Much better than last night." Of course, that didn't say much since she'd been mighty damn low.

"Good." She kicked a chunk of ice. "I'm sorry about your kid."

The ache with Evan's name on it threatened to overwhelm her, but she wouldn't let herself fall into a hole of forgetfulness again. She was stronger now. "Thank you, Emily. It's a scary time for me."

Emily swiped at the sludge with her boot again before backing away. "Guess I should go."

Dee reached through the window to grab Emily's elbow. Helping her would help Jacob, and he offered so few opportunities for anyone to give back to him. "No school today?"

Emily eased her arm free. "It's Saturday."

"Oh, right." Her life was such a mess she couldn't

keep the days of the week straight. Some candidate for straightening out a sullen teen. "Where's Chase?"

Emily studied a snowdrift. "Home, released to his parents who've locked him in his room for the rest of his life."

So much for pointing out Chase's brush with the police. Maybe a direct approach might be best. "I know it seems like your brother was rough on Chase last night, but Jacob would have been within his rights to do a lot worse."

What a mixed blessing to have regained her memory at such a horrible cost to Jacob and his sister.

Emily twirled the nursery monitor by the flexible antennae. "You wouldn't understand."

"Just think about seeing it from your brother's side. Jacob made the hard choice, even if it's tough to admit it." Dee gripped Emily's arm before she could bolt away. "I do understand how much it hurts when the man you love lets you down."

The teen blinked back tears and seemed ready to thaw... Then she backed away. "I gotta go help Grace pack Madison's stuff."

Part of Dee screamed Emily just needed time to reason through the crazy shift in their world. But she'd seen how a day of unresolved anger could stretch into years of alienation. Heaven knew she'd learned that lesson the hard way with her parents, a mistake she planned to fix as soon as she found Evan.

It was past time he met his grandparents. If only she hadn't waited too long. The regret would be unbearable.

She stepped out of the truck and charged after Emily. "Your brother loves you. I've seen that. He wants to help you but doesn't know how."

Emily spun on her heels, anger as bright as her unshed tears. "Sure he loves me. He just doesn't want a screw-up like me or Chase in his life. We're not all perfect like him, you know. Wait till you mess up, then you'll see. He'll dump you just like he's dumping me onto Grace."

The barb hit home and stuck like a prickly bur. Kids didn't fight fair. She should have remembered that from her teaching days.

Dee understood well enough how it felt to have a family member's disapproval, but Jacob was different. "He's not like your father." *Or mine.* "He's here for you."

He'd said Emily wanted to stay in Rockfish, the reason he wasn't taking her and the baby with him. Jacob took care of everyone.

But he never let anyone get too close to him.

Emily backed away. "I don't need this psychobabble crud from you. I'm outta here."

Intellectually Dee understood Emily was transferring her anger from Chase over to Jacob. Yet as Dee watched Jacob lope down the steps with a Thermos of coffee in hand, she couldn't help but remember Emily's words.

Such a perfectionist himself, how would Jacob accept failures from others? She had her fair share of flaws. Her perfectionist parents had frozen her out for years because of one mistake.

Climbing back inside the truck, Dee shook off her own emotional baggage and focused on Jacob. While in many ways a loner, he never turned his back on anyone in need. He took care of lost souls like herself—like his sister—on a regular basis. Yet how close did he allow himself to become in return? How much of himself did he share?

A woman could lean on those broad shoulders forever.

Would he ever lean on her?

She couldn't settle for less than everything from a man ever again. If she and Jacob didn't learn how to share control, find some balance between them, she feared she would lose Jacob as well as Evan. The chill inside her spread, and she couldn't seem to jam her feet under that heater enough to warm herself.

Jacob opened the driver's-side door, a blast of cold air gusting inside. Dee suddenly realized they would be alone together for the night.

When they arrived at the base's visitor's quarters, would they be staying in one room or two?

Chapter 15

Tossing aside his duffel bag next to the tiny micro-wave, Jacob wondered if Dee had expected him to get two rooms rather than one.

A moot point since he was lucky to have snagged even this last available visitor's quarter. She had been antsy and distant since he closed the door on the small space with a bed, a blue sofa and corner mini-kitchen. She would likely wear a hole in the carpet if she kept walking around.

Worries for her son, he could understand. He'd felt that radiating from her every pore when he'd held her while they'd watched the sun come up. This was dif-ferent.

She'd been so certain the Suburban hadn't gone into the river. Could she be doubting now? He didn't even want to think of what it would do to her if that body turned out to be her ex-husband.

He needed to calm her, if he only knew where to start. Right now, she'd taken to staring out the window as if she might find answers there.

Parents always wanted to talk about their children. He'd learned that from his friends and a woman he'd once dated who had a kid from a prior relationship.

He sat on the sofa and hoped that would encourage her to join him. "Tell me about Evan."

Dee's head swiveled away from the window toward Jacob. Pain glinted in her eyes like icicles on the bare oaks outside, then melted with her tender smile. "Evan loves chocolate ice cream and anything that flies. He has this plastic plane, a tub toy, that he's carried around forever, like his blanket." She sniffled and scrubbed the back of her wrist under her nose as she leaned against the wall. "I promised him a toy aircraft carrier for his birthday."

Her ache lanced at him with surprising force. He'd felt empathy before, but this was something more. Her pain was his. His investment in finding Evan became all the more personal. "We'll have another birthday for him with a huge cake and a trip to one of those places with goofy people in costumes, where kids can play video games."

How easily the word *we* slid from his mouth, bringing images of creating a normal family life.

"He would like that…. His birthday." Her hand fluttered to rest on her stomach. "He was an emergency C-section delivery. The placenta began to separate, and the doctor had to go in—" She blushed, staring at her crossed feet. "Oops, TMI."

"TMI?"

"Too much information." She tugged the hem of her sweater, molding cashmere to the gentle swell of her breasts. "You don't need to hear all the details."

Jacob waited for her to continue. He wouldn't let her shut down now that he finally had her talking.

Dee shoved away from the wall, pacing restlessly, straightening a basket with coffee essentials, nudging the duffel upright with her toe, straightening the bedspread. "I used to mourn having lost out on the childbirth experience. Now I thank God for that scar." She turned to Jacob. "It made me work harder at regaining my memory. Who knows how long I would have floated otherwise?"

"You're a stubborn lady." He admired the fortitude she had to possess in order to trudge through biting Rockfish winds to get back to the hotel after her ex had left her for dead on a deserted road. "I think you'd have punched through the fog before long."

Dee paused from evening out the mini-blinds to smile. "Thank you again for all you've done."

He didn't want her gratitude. What did he want? She was important to him. A couple of weeks ago he would have said too important and run like hell. "No thanks needed. And, Dee? We're going to find your son."

"You say that with such confidence. I envy your self-assurance." She crossed to the sofa and dropped to sit beside him. "I've made so many mistakes, Jacob—big screw-ups. I can't help but wonder if this is my punishment, that I've somehow brought this on myself and Evan's the one who will pay."

"We all make mistakes." He'd made his own fair share in not connecting with his sister. Hell, look at how he'd never managed a serious relationship in thirty-two years. "Worry about your child, cry for him, shout out your frustration. That's normal. But put the blame where it belongs. On Blane."

She shook her head in mute denial.

Jacob silently damned Blane Lambert to hell for making Dee so wary. Evan and Dee, and even Jacob, were all having to pay. "Mistakes are tough to accept, especially when the stakes are so high. I'm not giving up until I find him. You have to trust me to do this with you."

A spark fired in her eyes. "That's all great—" she held up a firm finger "—as long as I get to be an equal partner in reclaiming my life and my son. While I'm grateful for your help, I can't sit back and count on you to do everything for me. I need to take charge, to have some control."

She flattened her hand against his chest. Memories of making love to her rolled through his mind like a video on fast-forward. He wanted her again, but needed to think about her. She was going through hell right now, had to be suffering from huge emotional fallout

after all they'd learned at the police station and from
Spike.

Jacob stared at her hand on his chest. She might need
him to lay off, but then again, she might need the
comfort after hearing about the Suburban in the water,
the body near it.

He didn't even want to think about the implications
himself, so he couldn't imagine how torn up she had to
be. The air hung heavy between them as he looked back
down at her. "Do you want me to sleep on the sofa?"

A smile, her first today and not much of a smile at
that, but a definite tilt to her lips tipped into her cheeks
as she swayed toward him. Then he saw the heat, the
desire, the need to escape firing into her eyes.

"In the bed, with me," she said with conviction,
sliding her arms around his waist and tipping her face
in an unmistakable invitation for a kiss. "Or we could
stay here together on the sofa for now, the bed later."

"Good. Because that's exactly where I want to be."
He reminded himself now wasn't the time to talk about
futures when hers was so uncertain. All the same, he
couldn't help but want more from her. And the more he
wanted, the more he stood to lose.

She'd come full circle, starting in one small lodging
room, ending in another. Only this time, she wouldn't
let the world control her.

She'd meant what she'd said. She wanted to share his
room, Jacob's bed.

The thought threatened to scare the warmth right out of her. But her every maternal instinct screamed that her son was alive and she knew she was doing everything possible to find him, thanks to Jacob's help. She couldn't find Evan tonight, but she could soothe her heart and soul enough now to carry on the fight tomorrow when she might need every scrap of strength she possessed to cope with whatever they discovered.

Dee angled forward and found his mouth. Jacob looped his arms low around her waist. Kiss for kiss, he twined his tongue with hers, exploring, tasting, demanding.

She pressed against him until he relented and leaned back on the sofa. Anchoring him, she flattened her tender breasts to his chest, rolled her hips against his already rigid arousal. His hands reached for her shirt, and she shoved them away, pinning them to his sides. This was her show, her night to lose herself if only for a few hours.

Dee inched away from him, her mouth being the last thing to break contact. "Don't move."

His brows lowered over his moody eyes. He paused, then raised his hands in surrender. Layer by layer, she tossed aside his clothes, rediscovering every patch of his skin with her mouth until tendons strained along his neck.

Again Jacob reached for her. "Dee, enough."

And again she pushed aside his questing hands. "Not nearly."

"Well, hell," he growled. "Then it's my turn."

"Soon. We've still got the bed later."

Employing the same slow precision with which she'd tossed aside his clothes, she repeated with her own. None of her prior insecurities remained as she shrugged off her bra, stepped from her jeans and whisked away her panties. His gaze heated with appreciation as he watched, further firing her own need.

Dee scooped his pants from the floor and pulled free his wallet. A quick search uncovered just what she'd expected. He'd come prepared.

She plucked out the condom and braced her knees on either side of his hips. Dee clasped him, silencing him as she unrolled the condom with a languorous stroke.

Groaning, he palmed her back and brought her down to him, skin to skin for the first time in what felt like forever. Dee sighed, gently brushing herself along the tempting rasp of the hair on his chest—then gasped as his hands cupped her bottom.

"Enough," he said again, his voice leaving no room for argument.

They rolled from the sofa in a tangle of arms and legs. Jacob twisted at the last minute, and she landed on top of him.

Exactly where she wanted to be, in control.

She wriggled until her legs straddled him again. As she lifted to ease herself on him, he grabbed her hips. With a growl of frustration, she clasped his wrists and pinned his arms to the floor.

Dee took him inside her, control slipping elusively

away as the heat of him filled her. Jacob's jaw clenched as he battled for restraint. She reveled in pushing him to the edge before he'd even had a chance to touch her.

He shook his hands free of her grasp and filled them with her breasts, his thumbs circling her already pebble-tight peaks. She slid her hands over his and pressed while her hips rocked against him.

He palmed the small of Dee's back and began rolling her off him. She resisted. He braced a leg around hers and started to flip Dee to her back. Again, she resisted, her eyes sparking a mix of mischief and resolve.

He stroked her hair from her face, searching her eyes. "What do you want from me?"

"Everything."

Jacob hooked her leg over his hip and flipped her to her back in a smooth sweep that left her gasping, gripping his shoulders to secure herself the swirl of sensation.

He drove into her with powerful thrusts she met and equaled. She found new strength in his, new reserves she never knew she possessed.

Jacob reached between them and stroked her, teased her. "You're mine."

Dee tensed her leg around him, her body trembling with the force of powerful emotions she only just barely contained. "You're mine."

She watched her words register in his mind a second before she catapulted him over the edge, Jacob's hoarse shouts of completion sending an aftershock through her. Somewhere in her fogged brain, she heard him gasping, too.

Was he shaking or was she?

He gathered her to his chest, buried his face in her hair, and she wondered what the hell had just happened between them.

You're mine.

Her words or his? On a day filled with too many questions, she couldn't find the answer before sleep overwhelmed her.

The ringing alarm clock pulled Dee from sleep. She waited for Jacob to hit the snooze button, but the warm weight of his leg between hers didn't move. The steady beat of his heart thumped beneath her ear as she squinted against the morning light piercing through the mini-blinds.

Slowly the layers of grogginess peeled away and she realized it wasn't a clock, it was the—

"Phone, damn it." Jacob bolted upright and reached to snag the receiver. He scrubbed a hand over his face, then up to his mussed hair. "Jacob Stone here."

Dee gasped, sat up, praying he'd picked up in time. No one knew to call them here except for his friend with the OSI. Anyone else would have used his cell phone number.

She hugged the plaid cover to ward off the chill of the winter morning and abrupt wake-up after the night of warm comfort in Jacob's arms. Still, she was immediately alert. Tense. Waiting for any news of her little boy.

"Yeah," he barked into the receiver, paused, frowned, glanced at her with inscrutable eyes. "Uh-huh. Right. She's here with me."

Bad news? She prepped herself for the possibility the body in the river could be Blane's after all. She couldn't let herself think about the possibility they had found her precious son in those icy waters.

Even the thick swaddling of a bedspread couldn't ease the cold that thought brought.

She bit her lip to keep from asking questions. If she interrupted him, the information would only come slower from whoever had called.

Jacob extended the phone toward her. "It's Spike."

"The border patrol? He found something?" She could barely allow herself to hope everything could be resolved this quickly.

He shook his head. "Your home phone. Someone called and left a message, someone claiming to be Evan."

She forgot to breathe. Something she didn't realize until the room grew dim and Jacob grasped her arm. She gasped in air.

"Spike wants to play the tape over the phone for you to identify the voice."

Dee grabbed for the receiver and cradled it to her ear, a lifeline to her son. *Please, please, please.* "Agent Keagan? This is Dee Lambert. I'm ready whenever you are."

She kept her eyes focused on Jacob's face, needing the contact. The strength. Oh God, she couldn't face another letdown if this wasn't her baby boy.

"Yes, ma'am, hold on just a second while I patch through the recording."

A crackle sounded then cleared. "Mommy?"

The one word squeezed the air from her lungs. She gripped the phone as if she could somehow strengthen the connection.

"Mommy? I don't feel so good. Please come and get me...."

A dial tone echoed as the call faded away. A click sounded, followed by Keagan coming back on the line to ask her a question she could barely hear over the roaring in her head.

Now she couldn't stop breathing, gasping, shaking. She forced her lips to move. "It's him. It's Evan."

Chapter 16

He stared out his bedroom window at his parents' silver Suburban and wished like hell he could just drive away from here.

Chase punched his pillow and imagined he could sock Jacob Stone for putting him in this crappy situation. He flung the goose down lump away, envisioning it was Emily, getting the hell out of his life once and for all. No more trying to trap him with her clingy demands to spend time with her. He liked the kid, sure, but he just wasn't ready to be a dad yet. He wanted to play the field awhile longer. He was only just turning eighteen tomorrow, for God's sake. There were so many women out there.

Like Dee.

Man, she was hot and didn't even know it, a big part of her appeal. He flopped back on his bed, remembering the time he'd snuck into her room while she'd been bathing. He'd only wanted to freak her out a little to rattle Jacob. So he'd used some of his mom's lipstick to write on Dee's mirror.

He'd hoped to shake up Jacob and yeah, while he'd been watching, he'd seen the man get totally pissed off. He should have felt victorious.... But afterward, nothing had changed. Jacob hadn't bolted back to Charleston with Emily in tow. Chase's world was just as junked up as before and ready to explode.

For nearly a year the pressure in his head had built and built. He'd been about to break up with Emily this time last winter so he could go out with this other girl.

Then Emily had told him she was pregnant and now he had to make like he was a devoted dad when he was dying to bang this chick in his study hall. He could have walked away from Emily easily enough, though, at first, but his parents had put the screws to him about doing the right thing, blah, blah, blah.

He had to be free of her, and if that meant he had to leave the kid behind, too, then so be it. Now would be a good time to make his move, anyway, with all the local cops in a tizz because of Dee's ex-husband.

Lucky bastard. Nobody seemed able to turn up squat about him. The guy had done a kick-butt job of covering his tracks. Disappearing into thin air.

Chase sat up, an idea sparking. Maybe that's what

he should do. Screw it all and leave this place. Sure he would miss Madison, but it wasn't like the cops were letting him see her, anyway, since the misunderstanding at the Lodge. He'd only been helping himself to some money from the cash drawer, his due for things like shoveling the walk and helping out with the kid.

He swung his feet to the floor and opened his bedside table. There it was. His passport. He'd heard about tons of jobs with the oil pipelines coming out of Alaska. He could use the rest of the money he'd taken from the Lodge—enough for a bus or train ticket.

Eighteen tomorrow, he could start a new life in Canada, just like that "Mr. Smith" who'd been smart enough to offload his excess baggage.

And if Emily was wise, she would stay the hell out of his way or she would find herself in Dee's shoes—dumped for dead by the side of the road.

So close.

Squinting her eyes against the early morning sun, Dee could hardly believe her child had been so close all along. Less than an hour away according to the phone trace on the cell call that had gone through. Thank goodness Evan had left the phone turned on long enough for authorities to trace the location.

Amazing how little time it took these days, but then maybe Jacob's friend Spike really did know the "super-spy" tricks Crusty had credited him with. Her heart warmed whenever she thought about the outpouring of

support from those men she barely knew, men who'd dedi-
cated all their time and energy into helping her find Evan.

Now Jacob drove as fast as he could, given the
crummy conditions on the rutted, icy back road. The
police wanted her to go to the station and wait while
they pursued the matter.

Not a chance would she sit around. She was closer
to the target location than the police and her child had
said he was sick. Nothing would keep her from finding
him as quickly as possible. She gripped the EpiPen in
her pocket and prayed Blane hadn't accidentally fed
Evan anything with peanuts.

Dee was willing to meet authorities at the site—if she
could see Evan and reassure herself he was well. She
had to be there the minute they found her son. How
frightened he would be to ride in a cop car. As much as
she respected the local police, she knew the hoops they
had to jump through sometimes to stay within legal
boundaries. And frankly she didn't trust that they would
get their paperwork together before Blane had a chance
to bolt away. She couldn't take that chance with Evan's
life at stake.

Seconds whipped past with each jostle down the
weathered road deeper into the forest north of Rockfish.
Anticipation, tentative hope and more than a little fear
spiraled inside her as they drove deeper into the cluster
of icy firs. They hadn't seen a house in at least ten or
more minutes.

Jacob slowed, turning off the engine to coast silently

downhill as the seasonal road narrowed to nothing more than sludgy dirt.

Dee held up her hand. "I know. Don't get my hopes up." As if she could actually control that. Still, she tried to be logical so Jacob wouldn't worry about her wigging out. "It was just a cell call and the phone turned off shortly after that. They could be gone now."

He simply nodded, his eyes on the road, keeping his silence.

Even as they coasted, engine soundless, every crunch of the tires over the irregular road overly loud. She knew intellectually their approach was stealthy. Still, she couldn't stop wincing at every little noise.

When the clump of towering firs began to thin, he pressed the brakes and pulled out binoculars, scanning in the morning light filtering through the evergreen branches. She watched his expression for a hint....

His jaw flexed.

"What?" She couldn't keep the hope from her voice. "What do you see?"

He passed the binoculars to her. The casing still warm from his hands, she whipped them up to her eyes, pointed them where Jacob had looked last and found...

A blue truck with a camper attached to the back.

Someone was actually here, in the deserted area where a cell phone call had come through. Blane and Evan? The curtains were closed, so she had no way of knowing if anyone was inside, but still...

She prayed the camper didn't hold a group of

hunters. "I guess we have to wait for them to step out or for the police to show up."

"That would be wise." He reached to squeeze her arm before taking back the binoculars. "We can still watch. If they are inside and he tries to leave with Evan, we can stop him."

The conviction in his voice left her with no doubts. Jacob would die before letting her son get away again.

Die?

For the first time she realized she'd pulled him into a potentially lethal situation. Blane had already tried to kill her once, had tormented her with the lipstick incident. And she gave far more credence to those moments when she'd felt someone was watching her. But she knew Jacob wouldn't turn away now. She also knew he wouldn't be going into this alone.

Hopefully neither of them would if the police showed up soon.

Jacob sat up straighter in his seat.

"What do you see?" She tugged at his arm. Damn it, why hadn't he brought two sets of binoculars?

"Stay here." He turned to leave. "I'll be right back."

She grabbed his shoulder. "Sit here? You've got to be out of your mind. I've had enough of sitting and waiting to last a lifetime. Two lifetimes even." She thought of how often her parents had made all the decisions, and later how Blane had pushed her into the life he wanted for her. She wouldn't be shoved aside to a passive role any longer. "I will not lounge around while you play Rambo."

Jacob's mouth twitched in an almost grin.

Dee swatted his arm, frustration leaving her nerves tattered. "Don't laugh at me. I'm serious."

His face smoothed into genuine concern. "I know you are, but so am I. There's a man walking around, a guy wearing some kind of parka with a hood up, but he looks like your ex-husband."

She grabbed the binoculars from his hands and peered through until she saw…the back of a man in heavy winter gear. His height was right, but she couldn't tell anything more unless he faced her, which, damn it all, he didn't do before disappearing behind the camper.

She dropped the binoculars to her lap. "I can't tell if it's him."

Jacob reached for his door. "I'll try for a closer look, then." He turned back for the binoculars. "I'll be right back. I promise. Lock the doors."

She realized she wouldn't be able to sway him. And Evan might not be there, in which case she was wasting valuable time arguing with Jacob.

"Be careful." Dee flipped up the collar of his coat and kissed him, hard.

All the shared passion of the night before linked her to him. She could have sworn his kiss held the same for those hungry five seconds until he broke away.

Before she could find the breath to speak, Jacob ducked out of the truck and strode away. His boot prints in the snow left lengthy-strided reminders of his strength.

How long would she have to wait? Long enough to

go stir-crazy, no doubt. She eased her door open so she could listen better.

Wind whistled through the evergreens in gusts. Snow-laden branches swayed in a creaking dance over-head. The occasional icicle crackled, snapped, spiraled down to spike into the snow inches away from Jacob. He circled left, ducking around a fir. To her right, wind chimes tinkled on the breeze like a child's sweet laugh.

A child's laugh?

Dee held herself immobile and strained to listen, half certain her intense wishful thinking made her imag-ination play tricks on her. The high-pitched lilt sprin-kled the air again. Definitely a wind chime. Was there someone singing along in time? Her hope burned so in-tensely she worried about trusting her own ears.

She tipped her head to the wind and listened…. Again, she heard a young voice singing along. A strong, *healthy* voice. Her breath caught in her chest. Did Jacob hear, too, even though the voice came from the opposite direction he'd taken?

Dee's gaze skated left. Should she follow Jacob and tell him—or track the voice herself before it faded away?

She didn't even have to wait for the answer. Blane wasn't going to defeat "Dee" the way he had "Deirdre." She had to be there for Jacob *and* Evan.

Jacob had helped her trust herself, to take an active role in going after what she wanted. Never again would she be the Deirdre who'd run away from Blane so in-tensely she lost herself in the process.

Dee stepped from the truck. Her tennis shoes crunched against the hardpacked snow. She winced, as if Blane might hear and somehow know she'd come for their child.

Quit being ridiculous.

Dee picked her way through the sinister beauty of the frozen branches. The tinkling notes lured her closer, chimes and something else. Like those late-night infant whimpers and whispers that only a mother heard, each elusive sound sent Dee's maternal instincts on full-scale alert.

Then she heard it. Precisely. Chimes followed by the unmistakable giggle of a child.

Her child. Every cell within her cried out for her baby, a voice she'd recognized since hearing his first tiny wail.

Adrenaline pumped stinging heat through her as she wove past another fir. She ducked behind a towering trunk and listened. Again, Evan's laugh kissed the air. Dee pressed herself against the ice-slicked bark and peeked around.

Air whooshed from her lungs. Behind the camper where their binoculars couldn't have seen, Evan danced through the snow in his navy-blue snowsuit with energy and health to spare. Scooping up a fistful from a drift, he packed it into a ball and pitched it at the wind chimes abandoned on the branches of a twisted oak tree by some long-ago camper. He giggled as his aim proved true.

That laugh wrapped around her soul and squeezed. Love pounded through her with an intensity that rivaled labor contractions, along with a relief so intense she could hardly contain it all. Tears chased each other down her cheeks. Her arms ached with an emptiness she would soon fill.

Evan.

She almost bolted forward before she remembered the inherent danger. Where was Blane? And Jacob? Dee scanned the small clearing and found no one.

Adult-size boot prints left twisting paths, some older and half-filled with fresh snow. The deepest, most recent ones led to the cab of the vehicle. Through the window she saw…Blane was inside.

Cranking the engine.

He couldn't be leaving Evan. No way. He must be warming the car, in which case, time had run out for them. God, where was Jacob?

This could be it, a sliver of time to regain her child. If she waited for Jacob, Blane might come retrieve Evan before they could stop him. He could step out at any second.

She couldn't afford to wait. Tears froze on her cheeks as she sprinted from behind the tree trunk's protective cover. Her heart slammed against her ribs with each pounding footstep. Only a few more yards and she would have him.

Evan turned. His laugh rose into a squeal. "Mommy!"

What a beautiful word, a name she feared she would never hear again. Her arms locked around him and held tight. The sweet smell of him filled her senses.

"Evan!" Her breath hitched on a sob, and she hugged tighter. "I have you, baby. Mommy's got you."

"Missed you, Mommy." His sweet words puffed clouds into the subfreezing air. "You was gone a long time, so I snuck Daddy's phone away and called you."

With a familiarity that broke Dee's heart all over again, Evan clutched a lock of her hair and nuzzled it to his face. So often as a baby he'd done that very thing, like clasping a security blanket. How frightened and confused he must have been during his time away from her.

"I'm here now and nothing's going to make me leave again." The sound of the revving engine sent shivers down her spine. Blane was so close. Enough of happy reunions. She needed to get Evan away, fast. "We're gonna go for a ride."

"What about Daddy?" Evan glanced over his shoulder. He gripped her hair until she winced.

"Shh, sweetie," Dee whispered as she stumbled back toward the cluster of trees. Evan's extra weight threw her off balance. She forced herself to sacrifice speed for a more surefooted pace. The last thing she needed was to sprawl in the snow. "It's Mommy's turn to see you for a while."

"Okay." He smiled, innocently oblivious to the trauma all around him. "I was sick from the candy bar but Daddy gave me a sticky pin."

Thank God Blane had remembered about the extra Epis she always kept around Evan. "Good, that's great.

But I need you to be very quiet. We can talk all you want once we get to the truck."

Hugging her son closer, she started back toward where she'd come. If she could just make it back out of the clearing, she would have cover. Where was Jacob? Taking on life solo stunk. She could have used his clear-thinking steadiness.

And suddenly, there he was, tall, strong, dependable. Only a few yards away with his back to her he darted around a thick evergreen. Did she dare call out to him and risk alerting Blane? What choice did she have? She would have to take the chance.

"Jacob!" she called, gasping, stumbling as her feet hooked on a root. She twisted to protect Evan as she tumbled into the snow.

"Dee!" Jacob shouted as he broke through the trees, one arm outstretched. The dread on his face broadcast far greater concerns than a simple fall in the snow.

"Deirdre," a chilling voice echoed from behind her.

Chapter 17

Ten yards too far away to help, Jacob watched Dee tumble to the snow with her son clutched to her. A medium-build, blond man who matched Lambert's mug shot with eerie accuracy approached her, gun in hand.

Jacob felt as if his brain had been cleaved in two. One part of him assessed the situation with a calm of old. The other part urged him to fling himself on top of Dee and her child, shield them from the evil only three steps away. Why the hell had she left the truck?

"Deirdre," the man beside her called, each step toward her a menacing promise. He kept his eyes fixed on Jacob, his gun trained on Dee.

Her body jerked as if she'd been slapped. Dee's face

tightened and she squeezed her eyes shut as Evan whimpered in her arms.

"Blane." The whispered name carried a wealth of disillusionment. She curved her body protectively around a strong-limbed preschooler to keep him from seeing the gun.

Jacob absorbed the waves of pain radiating from her as if they were his own. And they were. He'd brought her here, to this. He'd promised to find her son and keep them safe.

Frustration and rage both slammed into him. And love. Hell, yeah, love.

He loved her so damned much his chest hurt with each icy breath. No more dodging the truth. What a time to figure it out.

Evan tipped up his face and thrust out his bottom lip. "Hurted my nose when we tripped."

"Sorry, sweetie." She clutched him tighter, pressing his face against her chest as if to comfort while keeping his eyes shielded from the horror unfolding. "We'll wash the scratch very soon."

Lambert closed in on Dee. "Well, my dear, imagine seeing you here, and with such a hulking companion. I thought you'd died out on that road, but you certainly landed on your feet—" he paused, gesturing with his gun to her crumpled in the snow "—figuratively speaking."

"Well, I'm very much alive," Dee answered through gritted teeth and poorly disguised fury. "Unlike that man in your Suburban in the river."

Blane shrugged. "Skidding away from you, I blew out my tires. I needed another ride that would be able to pull the trailer I'd already arranged to pick up. So I pulled over and pretended my car had broken down until the perfect Good Samaritan stopped by—one with a big truck."

The implication slapped over Jacob in an icy splash. Lambert had left Dee for dead, then hadn't hesitated to kill a total stranger just to steal his vehicle. The bastard was pure evil.

Then Jacob's brain snagged on an earlier part of the man's diatribe. Lambert had thought Dee died, too. But he had to know she was alive if he'd been stalking her at the Lodge. It didn't make sense.

Regardless, Jacob had to get the man the hell away from Dee and Evan. "Lambert, you want to deal with me. We don't want to risk the kid getting in the way."

"Of course not." He waggled the gun in his gloved hand. "Who says I'm going to shoot anyone? I just keep this around for protection against intruders. Right, Evan my boy?" His face creased with a wry smile. "Although a target as big as that fellow wouldn't be tough to hit if I wanted practice."

Jacob hoped Lambert *would* take a potshot at him, because then the gun would be away from Dee and Evan. If he could be certain the shot wouldn't be deadly and leave Dee without protection, he would rile Lambert into shooting now. "Go ahead then. You must have been itching to do this all those times you lurked around my place."

Lambert scowled. "What the hell are you talking about? The last thing I wanted was to see her again."

Jacob searched for words to stall the man until the police could arrive. "Then why not leave?"

"And live like some two-bit car thief on the lam? I hardly think so." He gripped Dee's arm and yanked her to her feet none too gently. "I'm waiting for my new ID to come through. I'd already started the process to get out of the country, but then Dee screwed up the time-table by digging through my old files. I just needed another couple of weeks to finish the transition of my assets into a shelf corporation so I would be free to travel under my new identity."

A "shelf corporation." Jacob narrowed his eyes with understanding. He'd heard of that. An old corporation with no activity was allowed to linger "on the shelf" until someone wanted to buy into it, usually to give age to a new business. Some had begun opting in to create a new holding for assets.

A crafty way to shield an old identity.

Lambert would have been able to conduct all trans-actions under the banner of his new company, his name never coming under the radar. He could have gotten clean away, losing himself in another country.

The possibilities shifted around in his mind. If the guy's explanation could be trusted, then who had followed them into Tacoma, and who tormented Dee that night at the hotel?

He'd been so sure when he'd seen the Suburban following them… One like the silver vehicle Chase's parents owned.

Hell. The realization exploded in his head. He had to trust that Emily would be safe with Grace's family because he didn't have the luxury of placing a timely call at the moment.

"Wait!" Dee reached up, her palm poised as an ineffective plug for the gun. Her eyes darted frantically between them. "Jacob, take Evan."

What the hell was she up to? He only knew he wanted her away from the barrel of that weapon. She really couldn't expect the man would let Jacob leave with the boy.

Jacob glanced at Evan. The sweet-faced kid had snuggled against Dee's breast. A sight so damned beautiful, Jacob struggled for air. Beautiful—except for the fact the kid was trembling, his confused eyes darting back and forth between his parents.

Dee inched away from Lambert and carried Evan toward Jacob—without a protest from Lambert. Why wasn't the guy stopping her?

Suddenly Jacob understood. Lambert honestly didn't want to frighten his kid. He didn't want his child seeing him shoot the boy's mother. This psychopath did love his son in a warped sort of way, and Dee had bargained on that to buy them time.

How long would it keep Dee safe? Only as long as she had Evan in her arms. The way the kid clung to his mother's neck, it didn't appear that he would let go anyway.

Jacob had to predict Lambert's next move, or he'd be left flatfooted and Dee could die. The fog of rage threatened to swallow him.

Concentrate. At least Lambert seemed content to keep up appearances for Evan and pay lip service to civility.

Where were the police? Spike had been leaving from the base, which meant he could be as much as forty-five minutes behind.

Jacob backed away from Lambert, his eyes never leaving Dee.

Dee pressed a kiss to her son's cheek. "I love you, sweetie."

"Love you, too, Mommy." His smile spread from ear to ear.

Dee's eyes met Jacob's and held. In the warm chocolate depths he saw trust and, God yes, love. Both directed at him at a time he couldn't afford to soak up the amazing beauty of the moment.

Then he saw a firm resolution that chilled him clean through. He could see she planned to—

Shove Evan toward Jacob with a twist of her body that placed her back completely to Lambert. She flung herself backward. Toward her ex-husband.

Directly in the path of his gun.

"No," Jacob shouted even as he wrapped his shoulders around her son, covered his face.

The gun exploded. Dee's body jerked, her eyes wide.

Blood staining her coat collar, she crumpled to the ground.

A roar of denial rolled through him. Jacob thrust Evan behind him and launched himself onto Lambert, throwing all the fury inside him into the charge. They stumbled backward, boots stamping for purchase on the packed ice. He rammed the bastard's arm against the camper with a satisfying snap. The gun dropped into the snow a second before Jacob downed Lambert. Their bodies slammed into a frozen snowdrift. It hurt. Not enough.

Lambert landed a gut punch with his uninjured fist and Jacob welcomed the reverberating pain that narrowed his focus. He steadied his vision. "This is for Dee, you son of a bitch."

He plowed his fist into Lambert's face. Twice. Lambert's eyes rolled back into his head as he sagged into unconsciousness.

Jacob held his fist aloft and resisted the urge to beat Lambert into a pulp. His rage demanded more than justice. He wanted revenge for Dee.

Dee. Reason pushed its way through the haze of fury.

He had to check her, get her to a doctor, but he couldn't risk Lambert coming to. Wasting a critical minute, Jacob hefted the man up and tossed him in the back of the camper. He jammed a branch across the back to lock him in.

"Dee?" Jacob shouted, racing to where she lay in the snow, Evan kneeling beside her, patting her face, crying, shell-shocked.

Jacob's hands skimmed her body. Where was the gunshot wound? His fingers settled on her neck. He found a pulse. Faint, thready, but beating.

Air gushed from his lungs.

Carefully, he opened her coat and found blood staining her sweater along her collarbone. He heard a crunch of snow behind him and stiffened, ready to go on the attack—only to see Evan eyeing him warily.

Jacob forced his face to smooth. "It's all right. I'm a friend of your mom's, and I'm going to take good care of her."

"Mommy? Mommy, wake up." Evan's voice shook.

No time to check the damage, he scooped her in his arms. "Your mommy's going to be fine, kiddo. Come on with me and we'll take her to the doctor."

Evan stared up at him with watery eyes. "What about my daddy?" His chin quivered. "He shot my mommy."

Jacob had tried his best to shield the boy. No child should have to see that. "Your father is resting inside." Of course the kid had no reason to trust him, a stranger. Jacob searched for the right words. "Remember how your mom wanted you to go with me? You need to do this for her."

He would carry them both if he had to, but he hoped it wouldn't come to that.

Evan's face cleared and he nodded, casting a frightened glance back at the camper. "Okay. It's Mommy's turn to have me for a while."

"Good job, kiddo." Jacob grabbed the keys from

Lambert's truck, just in case, and charged back into the woods with Dee cradled to his chest. He could get her to a hospital faster than any ambulance would find them out here.

He'd heard about domestic violence cases going wrong, but never had he expected to be in the middle of such a horror. His boots pounded through the snow, his pace slowed because of the child huffing alongside him. Dee's child. He would keep Evan safe for her.

And Emily. God, he couldn't wrap his brain around the notion that Chase had been so unbalanced, following Dee around, making threats. This could have been his sister and her child out here.

Hell, it could be his sister now.

Jacob neared the truck just as the police pulled up along with a Land Rover he recognized as belonging to Spike. Help had arrived. The police would take care of Lambert, and Jacob would make damn sure to tip off Spike about Chase so Emily and Madison would have protection ASAP.

Thank God with a blaring siren, one of the cops could get Dee to the hospital faster and he intended to be by her side the whole ride there, never letting her or her son out of his sight.

As he held her unconscious body in his arms, he just prayed it would be soon enough.

Dee grappled through layers of consciousness. No cottony amnesia fog for her. This felt more like digging through dirt to reach the surface of the life she desperately wanted to reclaim.

Could anyone sleep this deeply and ever awaken? How much easier it would be to stop struggling through the fog and—*ouch*. The pain socked her out of left field.

Only she couldn't stay asleep to hide from the ache. Her mind wrapped around her reasons for living, compelling reasons.

Jacob and Evan.

She battled, and pushed and fought her way back until a pinpoint of light beckoned. Prying her eyes open, she winced at the brightness and squeezed her lids shut again. Slowly, she eased them open, letting her pupils adjust to the rays streaming in through her half-open blinds.

Where was she? Panic slashed at her as she groped for answers. The antiseptic scent filled her nose. She looked around at what appeared to be a hospital room, searching for something, anything familiar.

Her gaze rested on a chair tucked in the corner of the room. A large hulk of a man sat cradling a small, sleeping boy in his arms.

Dee's world came sharply into focus. She remembered everything. Blane hadn't won. She recognized Jacob and Evan, two precious faces she would never forget.

Blane's attack, his threats, all came jumbled back with nauseating force. Dee studied every inch of Jacob, and he seemed unharmed. A sigh shuddered through her.

Jacob's eyes were closed. His head was tipped back against the reclining chair. Evan slept curled in his lap, chocolate ice cream staining the sides of her son's mouth. Jacob had obviously discovered the way to Evan's heart quickly.

Just as he'd done with hers.

She absorbed the image of them both and let the love fill her. Her still-slumberous mind wandered dreamy paths and she envisioned them as a family. The two looked nothing alike, Jacob so dark and angular, Evan so fair with a rounded face. Chances were Evan would never be as tall as Jacob.

No one would ever mistake Evan for Jacob's biological son. But with Jacob's influence, Evan would resemble Jacob in all the ways that counted.

She'd found so much beneath that brooding exterior. He'd shown her honor, constancy and a fierce protective love she hoped to claim.

Jacob shuffled, woke and stared back at her for seconds that seemed to stretch into forever before he spoke. "You okay?"

She nodded.

"I'll call the nurse."

"No, please. Give me a moment before the hospital frenzy takes over." Evan stirred, and she lowered her voice. She wasn't ready to share Jacob and Evan with the world, not yet. "What happened?"

He stood slowly, his big hands carrying her son with

gentle strength. "You were shot in the shoulder, but the bullet passed through without hitting anything vital."

She'd meant what happened with Blane, to Jacob to make him look so haggard, but now she realized those shadows under his eyes were for her.

"I'm okay," she reassured even though she actually felt more than a little weak and breathless. But alive. They were all alive. So she asked again, "What happened?"

"Blane is in custody."

She searched his eyes for details of how that must have happened, what had occurred after the shooting, and saw only a fierce protectiveness in Jacob's expression. She knew. He'd been there for her, for her son and for their future because here he stood vital and alive.

More details from the showdown spilled through her mind, of how Blane hadn't been the one stalking her. "What about Emily?" She struggled to sit up, her heart pounding. "Please say they have taken Chase back in for questioning."

Jacob nodded reassuringly. "It's okay. Take it easy. I was able to tip off Spike when he showed up a few minutes after you were shot. He took care of sending police over to Grace's right away. Chase is at the station now. Emily and Madison are fine. A little shaken up, but okay."

She sagged back on her pillow, relieved, somewhat drained, but mostly happy. It felt good to smile. To hope. She reached out her hand, twisting it free of the tangle of the IV to touch Jacob's arm. He held her sleeping son against his chest, Evan's arms draped over the broad shoulders as he tucked his face into Jacob's neck.

A sight she could enjoy forever. She skimmed from Jacob to her son and traced each tiny feature she'd feared never seeing again. The feel of baby-soft skin soothed her ragged nerves and a few of her fears. It would be a while yet before she could let him out of her sight.

Apparently Jacob had known that. Children in hospital rooms were usually a taboo. He must have executed some major arm-twisting for her to see Evan when she woke. "Thank you for having him here for me."

"No sweat."

"Yeah, right."

He shrugged.

A tap sounded on the door. Apparently their time alone would be cut short after all.

Emily peered around the door. "Dee? God, I can't believe… Wow, you're already awake." The teenager rushed to her side. "You're really awake. The nurse said…"

Jacob circled around to stand by his sister, more of that protectiveness radiating from him. "I haven't pressed the call button yet."

Emily flipped her ponytail over her shoulder, shifting from foot to foot. "I won't stay long. Grace has Madison and she's really kind of a handful today, so I need to get back to her. I just had to see you." Her gaze slid up to her brother. "And you, too."

A corner of his mouth tipped. "You're speaking to me now, are you?"

She clutched the bedrail in a white-knuckled grip. "The police are talking to Chase again. He showed up at Grace's house and the cops were only a minute behind him." Guilt, frustration—pain—all mingled in her blue eyes the same color as Jacob's. "I heard him admit to stalking you, Dee."

Jacob secured Evan against his shoulder, his eyebrows pinching in sympathy. "I'm sorry this had to happen."

"Me, too." Emily picked at Dee's hospital blanket. "It's tough, isn't it? Loving somebody only to find out he isn't who you thought he was."

Dee covered the girl's hand with her own. "Yes, sweetie, it is."

Emily allowed the comfort long enough for a nurse's cart to rattle past before a half smile reached her lips if not her eyes just yet. "Your kid's really cute."

"So's yours." Dee ached from more than the gunshot wound as she thought of that little baby without a reliable father.

Emily's smile faltered. "This mother thing is tough to do alone."

Dee nodded and waited for Jacob to speak up, willed him to step in and be the kind of brother, support, family Emily needed. He needed them, too, even if he didn't realize it yet.

She stared between the two stubborn siblings....

Jacob cleared his throat, his stance still assertive,

pushy even, but his eyes gentle. "I can get a transfer to Tacoma, but it wouldn't come through until the summer. You know the courts aren't going to let you live alone, but I want you to have choices. I can pay Grace to stay with you until I move here, or you can come with me to Charleston. I have friends there who would help out while I'm TDY."

Dee wanted to be a part of the picture, but knew it was too soon to have those sorts of expectations from a man she'd known all of a couple of weeks.

A man she'd already grown to love more than she'd realized was possible. But a love formed with wide-open eyes and a wiser heart this go-round.

Emily braced her shoulders, her chin high, and for the first time, Dee could see the family resemblance in these two strong-willed siblings.

The teen tossed her head, her ponytail swishing with its red stripe of defiance glinting. "There's nothing for me around here anymore. If you really don't mind having us, Madison and I will go with you."

"Good. Good." Jacob secured Evan with one arm and reached to pull Emily to him with the other.

Dee heard a couple of whispered words go back and forth that sounded a lot like "love you, kiddo" and "love you, too" before Emily pulled back with overly bright eyes to match her grin.

"I'll leave you two—or three—alone." Emily smoothed a hand over Evan's head before backing away. "Definitely a cute kid."

The door swished closed behind her.

Dee pressed a kiss to her hand then her fingers to Evan's forehead. She wanted to hold him. If only she weren't so unsteady. She needed to gather him up and rock him as she'd done so many times before.

Thanks to Jacob, she would have that chance. "You could set him on the recliner and let him sleep while we talk. I need to hear more about what happened, starting with Chase."

Jacob lowered Evan back to the recliner, then returned to Dee's bedside.

She pushed herself up to her elbows and raised the bed. Jacob stuffed his hands in his jean pockets, looking so tall and strong. If only he would reach down and take her hand.

"Spike *and* the cops showed up right after the shooting. As I said, I tipped off Spike about Chase as we were loading you into the police cruiser to come to the hospital. Lambert is in custody. With kidnapping and assault charges pending—not to mention investigating the murder of the man in the river—Lambert won't be out anytime soon. They'll have plenty of time to make a solid case about his role in defrauding the airplane manufacturers."

It wasn't the way she'd ever envisioned her marriage ending, but at least she and Evan were safe. Thanks to Jacob.

She scoured Jacob for signs of injury. "Are you sure you're all right?"

His hand fell to rest on her shoulder, warm and heavy. "Just a couple of bruised ribs." He waved aside her concern. "I thought there was no way we could all walk out alive. But together, we pulled it off."

"We?"

"You and me." He lowered the bedrail and sat beside her.

Her pride be damned, she had to know how he felt, where she fit into all of his plans with moving and Emily. "I love you, Jacob. I know it's only been a couple of weeks, but I've never been so sure of anything in my life."

He pressed a finger to her lips. "You don't have to explain it to me. I understand. Sure, we've only known each other a short while. But for me, it's more than long enough to be sure I love you, too. I want to be with you and take the time to show you just how much." His eyes narrowed with intensity. "I don't want to stuff away my feelings until they freeze up like my old man's."

She curved her hand to his cheek. "You're nothing like your father. You're the most giving man I've ever met. If anything, I wish you would let me do more for you, let me know what *you* need."

Jacob's face tightened as if the next words pained him. "I need you. I need your stubborn, sometimes bossy, grab-life attitude. Military relationships are tough, with long separations, the stress of dangerous deployments—"

This time she pressed a finger to his lips. "I've been

through the toughest situation possible. I believe I can handle anything as long as we're in it together, partners."

His mouth curved under her touch. "That's a promise I can easily keep."

She tipped her face to his. Their lips met, and she felt the love, a total giving and acceptance of self flow between them.

Passion was easy, an emotion that carried them away. The tender give-and-take of their kiss, however, was a hard-won gift, one she would never take for granted.

He cupped her face in one hand. "So you and Evan will come to Charleston with me until I get a transfer back here?"

"Charleston or Tacoma, it doesn't matter as long as we're all together."

He reached into his pocket and pulled out her tarnished gold necklace. The *D* glinted in the fluorescent lighting of the hospital room. "The nurse gave me this when they checked you in."

Jacob leaned forward, slid it around her neck. "Lean forward and I'll hook it for you, Deirdre."

She glanced down at the necklace and read the letter. "'Dee.' I'm Dee. This time I know who I am."

His smile grazed across her lips with the promise of a future full of love, children and sunsets. A future full of memories just waiting to be minted.

* * * * *

Be sure to catch Catherine Mann's new series,
THE LANDIS BROTHERS,
launching this May in Silhouette Desire.

NEW YORK TIMES BESTSELLING AUTHOR

DIANA PALMER

A brand-new Long, Tall Texans novel

IRON COWBOY

*Available March 2008
wherever you buy books.*

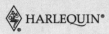

HARLEQUIN®

INTRIGUE®

THRILLER—
**Heart-pounding romance and suspense
that will thrill you long into the night....**

Experience the new THRILLER miniseries
beginning in March with:

WYOMING
MANHUNT

BY

ANN VOSS
PETERSON

Riding horseback through the Wyoming wilderness
was supposed to be the trip of a lifetime for
Shanna Clarke. Instead she finds herself running
for her life. Only rancher Jace Lantry can
help her find justice—and serve revenge.

*Available in March
wherever you buy books.*

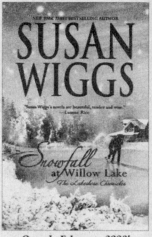

HARLEQUIN

Super Romance

Bundles of Joy—
coming next month to Superromance

Experience the romance, excitement and joy with 6 heartwarming titles.

BABY, I'M YOURS #1476 by *Carrie Weaver*

ANOTHER MAN'S BABY
(The Tulanes of Tennessee)
#1477 by *Kay Stockham*

THE MARINE'S BABY (9 Months Later)
#1478 by *Rogenna Brewer*

BE MY BABIES (Twins)
#1479 by *Kathryn Shay*

THE DIAPER DIARIES (Suddenly a Parent)
#1480 by *Abby Gaines*

HAVING JUSTIN'S BABY (A Little Secret)
#1481 by *Pamela Bauer*

Exciting, Emotional and Unexpected!

*Look for these Superromance titles in March 2008.
Available wherever books are sold.*

HARLEQUIN® Romance®

MEDITERRANEAN DADS

In the first of this emotional Mediterranean Dads duet,
nanny Julie is whisked away to a palatial Italian villa,
but she feels completely out of place in Massimo's
glamorous world. Her biggest challenge, though, is
ignoring her attraction to the brooding tycoon.

Look for

The Italian Tycoon and the Nanny

by Rebecca Winters

in March wherever you buy books.

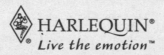

HARLEQUIN®
Live the emotion™

Silhouette®
Romantic
SUSPENSE

COMING NEXT MONTH

#1503 A DOCTOR'S SECRET—Marie Ferrarella
The Doctors Pulaski
Dr. Tania Pulaski vows never to get involved with a patient. Then Jesse Steele enters her ER. Although he's strong and attractive, she hesitates taking things to the next level…until someone starts stalking her and she must trust the one man who can help her.

#1504 THE REBEL PRINCE—Nina Bruhns
Serenity Woodson knows the charismatic and sexy man who's been helping her aunt must be a con man. Then she learns the incredible truth—Carch Sunstryker is a prince from another planet, on a mission to Earth that may save his kingdom. Loving him would be insanity—but neither can resist the intense attraction that could destroy them both.

#1505 THE HEART OF A RENEGADE—Loreth Anne White
Shadow Soldiers
After Luke Stone fails to protect his wife and unborn child, he refuses to take on another bodyguard assignment. But when he becomes the only man who can protect foreign correspondent Jessica Chan from death, he faces the biggest challenge of his life…because being so close to Jessica threatens to break his defenses.

#1506 OPERATION: RESCUE—Anne Woodard
Derrick Marx will do anything to rescue his brother from the terrorists holding him captive, including kidnapping the reclusive botanist whose knowledge of the jungle is the key to his success. Against her will, Elizabeth Bradshaw leads Derrick through the jungle, but quickly finds the forced intimacy is more dangerous than the terrorists themselves.

SRSCNM0208